Mistflower, The Loneliest Mouse

T0385716

Mistflower, The Loneliest Mouse

Krystina Kellingly

OUR STREET
BOOKS

Winchester, UK
Washington, USA

First published by Our Street Books, 2013
Our Street Books is an imprint of John Hunt Publishing Ltd., Laurel House, Station Approach,
Alresford, Hants, SO24 9JH, UK
office1@jhpbooks.net
www.johnhuntpublishing.com
www.ourstreet-books.com

For distributor details and how to order please visit the 'Ordering' section on our website.

Text copyright: Krystina Kellingley 2012

ISBN: 978 1 78099 468 0

A CIP catalogue record for this book is available from the British Library.

Design: Stuart Davies

Illustrations by Sarah Frances Nash

Printed and bound by CPI Group (UK) Ltd, Croydon, CR0 4YY

We operate a distinctive and ethical publishing philosophy in all
areas of our business, from our global network of authors to
production and worldwide distribution.

CONTENTS

TO NICK AND DANIEL

My beloved sons, who are undoubtedly
the best things I ever created
With all my love

Acknowledgements

Firstly I would like to thank my lovely son, Nick, for his unfailing belief in me over the years and for all the hours spent, reading, editing and commenting on my writing. Thanks, Nick, I would never have got here without you. Special thanks also go to my dear friend, Maria, without whose encouragement and belief this book would never have been written. Thanks also to my good friend, Carol for all her support and encouragement.

The Gathering

It was Walpurgis Night in Michaelmas Wood and as they always did, all the animals gathered in the clearing. Tonight, Ghost, the barn owl would lead the meeting. On this one night of the year no creature, no matter how small, need fear another.

But this Walpurgis Night an ill wind rode the skies – and as everyone knows – an ill wind never blows anyone any good. High above the rooftops, higher even than the tallest of tree tops, he gusted fitfully here and there, searching for a path to follow. He tore at clouds, lashed at branches and rattled windows. Finally he settled on his course and howled northwards.

* * *

'Gotcha!' Silk mewed, as he gently batted the bumblebee. He sprinted for cover and an instant later he was squeezing himself beneath the low branches of a Leylandii hedge.

'Not fair!' buzzed the bee. 'I can't get under all those thick, heavy branches.'

The little black and white kitten and the young bumble bee had been playing tag for quite some time. They had chased each other up and down the road where Silk lived for a while but they had long since left his home far behind.

Wrapped up in their play, neither of them noticed as the ill wind passed over, pausing only long enough to huff at them spitefully. They both felt its passing though and their high spirits disappeared as chill fingers snatched at them.

They glanced around realising that while they had been playing, the Sun had gone to sleep and the Moon was getting ready to rise.

The young bee found himself strangely afraid. He hovered in place, buzzing quietly. All of a sudden he wanted to be home, safe and sound in his nest.

'I – I'm going now,' he told his new friend. 'Bye.' And with that he hastily flew off.

The little kitten also found himself oddly troubled and wishing he were back home, curled up in his warm and comfortable basket. He peered around looking for the trail … but nothing seemed familiar. He didn't know which way to go.

Really scared now, he dashed first up this street and then down that road, before trying another. His heart was thumping hard in his chest and a frightened little mew escaped him as he darted about only to stop, disappointed and more and more panicky.

His stomach growled hungrily and the sky darkened overhead as he ran and ran and ran, searching and searching, until the Moon sailed forth from behind a cloud, hanging so low that when he paused in his frantic running, he could clearly see her cold and beautiful face looking down at him.

Perhaps, he thought desperately, the bee might be able to show him the way home. But his friend was nowhere to be seen. Still, Silk was sure he could remember the direction he had flown off in. Determined, the little kitten set off, doing his best to ignore the hunger pangs in his belly and the fear gnawing at his chest.

What seemed to him a very long time later, when he was almost too tired to stay on his paws and much too tired to fight off the fear any more, he saw a group of humans standing a little way down the street. His heart leapt for joy. They would know! They would be able to show him the way home. Of course they would. With his last burst of energy he dashed toward them mewing as he ran, telling them all about what had happened and how he came to be so lost.

Close to, he saw it was a group of young men – just for an instant he paused. Something in him telling him – *no*! *Don't go there*! But Silk ignored it. He trusted humans. He loved his own humans dearly, almost as much as he loved his mommy and they had never been anything but good to them both.

'Oh! Thank goodness, I've found you,' he mewed, relieved, winding himself in and out between their legs, hugging them with his tail. 'I was so scared! I've never been so far from home before. I've never been out so late. You'll help me, won't you? You—'

One of the youths reached down and grabbed him by the scruff of his neck, hauling him up and letting him dangle just level with his face.

'Well – look what we've got us here!'

'Y-you'll help me, won't you?' Silk mewed, suddenly very nervous. There was something about the boy's voice and the way he was looking at him that he didn't like. He wished he'd listened to that thing inside him when it told him no. But it was too late.

He hung miserably in the boy's grip. His heart was pounding hard again and now all he wanted was for them to let him go.

'*Please*!' He meowed. 'Please – don't hurt me.'

* * *

Mistflower, the mouse, had been one of the first to arrive. She glanced around herself, hearing soft rustlings and scamperings in the hedgerows and trees. If she strained her eyes and ears she could make out the slip and glide of a slow worm and several earthworms making their way to the gathering.

To each side of her, as well as overhead, gleaming pairs of eyes shone through the leaves and blinked on and off in the grass. Everyone who could get there would be here, she knew. Even the animals that were normally fast asleep by now would come.

She glanced up just in time to see a whole flock of starlings alight in the big old oak, in the centre of the clearing.

Mistflower could feel her excitement growing, singing in her whiskers and twirling through her tail. She loved this night above all others but there was a sadness mixed in with her pleasure. This was the first gathering she had attended alone and quite suddenly she found herself lost in thought, her bright eyes glittering as she remembered.

She had once heard somewhere, though she couldn't remember where, that people had a saying, 'poor as a church mouse', but she couldn't understand it at all. She supposed it had something to do with the fact there wasn't much in the way of food to be had in a church. But every church had a vicarage and the meals there were good and plentiful.

And Sage, ahh! She missed Sage most of all. A wise and loving mouse, and very much in demand in his younger days, she had never understood why he had chosen her. Her eyes softened, filling with tears. Sage had been everything to her and the pain of losing him was still as sharp now as it had ever been.

Who could have known back then how things would change? She didn't know why, but slowly people stopped coming to the church until, finally, no one at all came any more.

She missed the singing and the sound of the organ. She missed the children's choir; their voices had been so fresh, so full of hope. Mistflower loved children, her own and the sons and daughters of men, even though she knew full well she and her kind were not loved in return.

She had particularly enjoyed Christmas. She loved the joyful Christmas hymns and the magical story of the wonderful, special, baby. She thought someone like that, someone so gentle and kind and so great, would surely have found love in his heart, even for a despised mouse.

After all, it was The Great God of all living creatures Himself who had put her kind in the world. Mice were in the weave of the pattern and had their part to play.

Finally, when the very last creature had arrived and an expectant hush had fallen over the assembly and all eyes lifted to the heavens, Mistflower saw the pale shape of Ghost glide in on soundless wings.

No sooner had Ghost arranged himself comfortably in a deep V of the oak than he began to speak.

'So, the wheel turns and brings us once more to Walpurgis Eve. And a clear, crisp one it is. Night has spread her dark shawl over Father Sky and her brothers and sisters, the Stars, have come out to decorate it.

'See how they sparkle and how Mistress Moon lights our path.' Ghost turned his head surveying the creatures, great and small, gathered before him.

'Welcome all.' He blinked his big, luminous eyes. 'Welcome.

'First, as always, we will pay respect to the Great God of All Things and give thanks for life. After that I will listen to any matters of disagreement, as well as any crimes against our Law.'

The Law had been put in place at the time of Creation; it commanded every creature not to take more from any other creature, or from Mother Earth, than they had need of. It was a serious thing indeed to break the Law.

'Lastly, when all has been dealt with satisfactorily, we will have some sharing time.'

Mistflower curled her tail, content. Settling herself comfortably she waited for events to begin.

Soon it was time for the best part of the evening – the sharing. Mistflower waited with equal parts of joy and sorrow for Ghost to tell his story because once it was finished, the gathering would break up and all would head for home and that would be the end of it for another year.

Suddenly, Ghost began to speak. 'Once upon a time, in a place, far, far away, lived a deer named Windspark.

'Windspark was a very beautiful and graceful creature and she had many who loved her. But from the first time Windspark had glimpsed them, she loved only the stars. Every night when the other deer slept, Windspark would gaze up at Night's shawl and long to be amongst the glittering brothers and sisters. Finally, The Great God took pity on her and one night drew her up into the sky.

'At first, Windspark's heart was satisfied and she ran and played, dipping her hooves into the Milky Way, roaming the four directions with The Great Bear and sliding around the Moon on the tail of Draco, The Great Serpent.

'After a time though, her spirit grew heavy and she realised she missed her mother and her father. She missed the warmth of the herd and the simple pleasures of sweet grass and the cool, fresh water of the little river that flowed through their forest.

'The worst of it was, try though she might, by the time her mother and the rest of the herd had risen, Windspark and the stars had set. Sorrowfully, Windspark realised she was fated never to see her family or her friends again.

'One night, when Windspark felt her heart would break from longing, The Great God, who knows all, came to her.

'"What is it, Windspark?" The Great God asked. "Why are you so unhappy?"

'Windspark sighed. "I'm just sitting here thinking how very foolish I've been. I had so much and I took it all for granted and instead of being thankful, I wasted my time wanting something different and now I wish I was back where I started."

Windspark's soft, brown eyes flowed with tears.

'"Ahh!" said The Great God. "So you have been foolish, little one, and now you are wiser."

'"Maybe," Windspark said, "for all the good it'll do me."

'"Once, when the world was young, little Windspark," spoke The Great God, "and you were only a seed upon the winds of creation, you played where you would. Time was of no importance. But as your life spark became wiser, out of your love for me, you asked if there was something for you to do. So I sent you to Mother Earth in order that she could grow you. But you did not drink enough from the waters of forgetfulness and you longed for your home in the heavens."

'The Great God laughed and a cloud of butterflies, with colours as bright as the jewels Mother Earth gives up to those who desire them, arose from his breath. "And now you are here, part of you has remembered what it was you were meant to do, little one, and you wish to take up your task again."

'Once more, The Great, all loving, God took pity on lonely little Windspark and in the blink of an eye set her back in the exact same spot from which she had been taken up.

'In the morning there was great excitement and happiness when Windspark was reunited with her family and friends.

'Never again did Windspark long for something other than what she had. She had come to understand, each creature has its own path and achieving a great desire can sometimes come at too high a cost.'

There was silence among the animals for a little while as everyone thought over the story they had just heard. But soon enough, everyone said their thanks to Ghost and their goodbye's and started to gather themselves for the journey home.

In a few moments, Mistflower found herself all alone in the dark.

* * *

'Hate cats,' the boy said, his hard eyes locked on the little kitten dangling helplessly from his grasp. 'Vermin! Bad as rats. Dirty, filthy things.'

He glanced around, spotting a plastic carrier bag poking out from another lad's pocket. 'Here,' he held out his hand. 'Gimme me that.'

The lad took another swig from the vodka bottle he was nursing before wordlessly passing over the bag.

Silk suddenly realised he was in trouble. Giving a long eerie yowl, he clawed desperately at the hand holding him prisoner.

'Stop that!' The hand tightened its grip on him so he could hardly breathe and shook him hard until his head spun and his eyes rolled around in his head. By the time he had his wits back he was already inside the plastic bag and someone was tying the handles together, tight.

The next instant he found himself being whirled round and around.

'One. Two.' It was the boy's voice – the one who had shaken him and almost strangled him. He could hear someone else laughing. ' Three. Whheeeee!

One moment he was flying. The next, all the air whooshed out of his lungs as he landed heavily. He lay still, trembling, gripped with fear that the boys were standing over him, waiting for him to move, only to do it all again; whirl him round and around and then let him go, let him hit the ground all over again. It came to Silk that they meant to kill him.

Silk lay there, waiting. Nothing moved. Everything was silent and when he had calmed down enough to be able to pay attention to his senses, he knew the boys were no longer there. He was alone. For a short space of time he relaxed ... until he realised it was quickly becoming hard to breathe!

The Web of Time

Mistflower scurried back to her house thinking how true it was that the very thing you long for above all else and that makes you so happy when you get it, can then turn around and make you so miserable.

The days stretched lazily into summer and Mistflower kept busy. The long hours of daylight were easy to fill. In the light evenings, Mistflower liked to spend some time in the company of her friends. She especially liked to spend time with Gale, the pigeon.

Gale always had news and stories to tell. His great, great, great, grandfather had been in the army during the war and sometimes Gale would tell her about the brave things Granddad had done while carrying out his duties, delivering messages from one camp to another.

'The skies were full of biting things,' he'd say. 'Terrible things. With one snap they could kill a pigeon stone dead. Just like that. And Granddad would fly through them, dodging this way and that way. High times, Mistflower,' he would coo. 'High times. Exciting times.'

Summer was a happy and sociable time.

All too soon though, there was the smell of autumn in the air and suddenly the summer ease disappeared and every creature seemed to be preoccupied with matters that needed seeing to before winter set in. The birds repaired their nests and those who could gathered provisions.

Mistflower's small, leathery nose twitched, her whiskers dancing nervously as she peered cautiously around the corner of the cobbled alley. Directly across from her lay Farmer John's long wheat field. Mistflower could smell the crisp, nutty ears of wheat as the warm wind combed through them.

She sighed, steeling herself to plunge into the dense crop. For what seemed to her the hundredth time in the past few days, she wished she had someone to help her in her task of gathering provisions for the coming winter. She knew it would be a hard one and if she didn't work now, she would go hungry.

She dashed into the road without so much as glancing left or right. The Great God must have been looking out for her however, because she reached the edge of Farmer John's field on the other side of the lane, without so much as hearing the sound of anything coming.

Mistflower didn't even pause, running straight up the nearest ear of wheat and nibbling away determinedly until her cheeks were full. This, she decided, would be her final trip today. Tomorrow, she would make a few more forays and that should hopefully be enough to see her through winter.

It was getting dark by the time she once more reached the lane. Huge pairs of fiery eyes bore down on her, reminding her of the day Sage died, making her tiny heart pitter-patter and sending a spasm of fear through her body.

She blamed herself. After the children moved away, when Sage had gradually stopped being able to see, awful though that was, it had brought the two of them even closer. They had simply started doing everything together. Everywhere they went, Sage would hold onto her tail and in no time at all, it seemed as if they had never done anything differently.

She would lead Sage to the very best spot along the bramble bush and then go off to collect her own berries and Sage would eat his fill, picking the plump blackberries until he could eat no more.

She would collect him when her own harvesting was done and back home they would go, Sage once more holding onto her tail.

Mistflower's small furry body trembled like a downy duck feather carried on the breath of the North Wind. A soft anguished squeak escaped her. It had all worked perfectly well for the longest time; until that fateful, terrible day.

They had picked and eaten their fill and were on their way home. They had been almost halfway across when the Great God had stopped favouring them and in the dim light of a closing day she hadn't spotted the pool of oil on the black tar macadam road.

She had lost her footing, slipped and slid in one direction, while her beloved, her heart's light, lost his grip and was suddenly … *gone*!

She remembered, her breath, ragged in her throat; slipping, sliding, covered in oil. The dreadful, thrumming, rumbling mutter, getting louder and louder until it filled up her ears and head with its hard, inescapable sound. The blinding glare of the fiery eyes … and then … it was past … gone … and there was only silence and the pounding of her heart.

It had grown dark as she searched, calling for Sage and on The Great God. She had heard the hoot of an owl and once she had heard the strong beat of its wings close by. But she would not – could not, give up. Finally, she had found him. Unmoving, the light already faded from his unseeing, ever loving, gentle eyes.

She had lost her wits then for a little while, running around

Sage's body in circles, her grief driving her on.

It was Moss the Vole who had helped her, staying with her and speaking to her softly until she finally paused in her endless circling and began gathering her senses.

'There now, Mistflower,' Moss had comforted. 'The Great God must surely have loved Sage very much. And because he was such a wise mouse, he needed Sage to help him in his Great works. And though He knew how much it would pain you, he had to call for him.'

At last, Mistflower had let herself be calmed and though she felt as if her heart must surely be bleeding, she had followed Moss home.

Moss was gone now but Mistflower thought of her often, remembering her kindness.

This time, she made herself look right and left before hurrying across the road and back up the cobbled alley, under the fence, through the overgrown garden, slipping finally into the familiar worn space, beneath the faded green door.

Once indoors, she went straight to the little hole in the bottom of the skirting board — in the corner of the kitchen, behind the old pine wood table the housekeeper used to keep covered with a white lace cloth.

She stacked her latest hoard of wheat kernels with those she had already collected, quickly but thoroughly, she cleaned her nest before washing her face and paws.

Finished, she curled herself up into a little ball. The loneliness she carried with her, like a thorn in her soft heart, pressed down on her as it always did at the end of a day and as she always did, before fleeing from its torment into sleep, Mistflower offered up a prayer to the Great God that she might in some way be delivered up from her overwhelming loneliness.

She did not presume to dictate to the All Mighty how, when, or why. She simply put all of her considerable love into willing it and humbly asked that it might be.

She awoke to the muffled patter of fat, juicy raindrops against the kitchen window panes. Her button nose twitched at the burst of watery freshness carried by the downpour.

She had slept well and after a breakfast of oats and berries, she set off to finish collecting wheat for the winter.

* * *

Silk shivered and sneezed for the third time. The yew tree he was sat under offered him some protection from the sleeting rain but the grass was damp and enough wet got through to have left him soaked to the skin. His stomach growled but he barely noticed; hunger had become his constant companion.

He wished, as he had every moment since getting out of that bag, he hadn't gone away from his street that day. He wished he had never even set a paw outside the garden gate. He missed his mommy so much – and he was so lonely he thought he might die of it.

A few times, as he wandered around miserably, he had come across people but he had run away and hidden. He no longer believed he could trust all humans. He had stayed away from houses for the same reason. Until today, until he had come across the old house with its overgrown garden.

His nose told him no people lived here but still Silk was wary. There would be no more rushing in blindly. He would take his time, once he was sure there were no humans, he would see if he could find somewhere, some small space, where a kitten might be able to lie down and sleep, out of the cold and rain, even if only for a short spell.

Hard Choices

It was Mistflower's final trip and she had reached the undergrowth around the crab-apple tree when she was shocked into stillness, one paw in the air, everything from her tiny, pink nose to the tip of her long banded tail, frozen. Completely overcome by the strong and immediate odour of ... *CAT!*

As she stared, her horrified eyes settled on first ... a paw ... followed by another ... and close behind the paws came ... legs ... a body ... and last of all ... a head, emerging from around the tree trunk.

Mistflower ran for her life. Between her and the safety of the kitchen door lay the bare level surface of the garden path. She slowed to a stop, cowering beneath a broad leafed dock. Her lungs felt as if they were bursting and her breath scorched her fear constricted throat.

She crouched beneath the leaves, torn between running and staying where she was, expecting, at any minute the cat to bear down on her and crunch her up in its sharp teeth.

How long she trembled there, she would never know. It could

have been seconds or long, slow minutes before she was able to collect herself enough to realise that far from pouncing on her, the kitten, because that she realised was indeed what it was, simply sat on its haunches in the exact spot she had first seen it.

Actually, she saw it was really a very small kitten. But then, she shuddered, they were often the worst. They loved to play and would torment a mouse to death!

What was wrong with it anyway? Why was it just sitting there? Doing nothing. What was it waiting for?

Suddenly, she became aware of a strange sound. A sound that was ... was it ... it *was*! The kitten was crying!

Mistflower was caught, held by the kitten's unhappiness. As she listened, she realised its distress was growing. Despite herself, despite the fact cats and mice were sworn enemies, her soft little heart was troubled by the scruffy kitten's plaintive mewing.

But what could she do? She was after all, only a mouse. Even though the kitten was small, it towered over her. If she did try to help, it would only turn on her and, she shuddered again, it would surely kill her.

The sensible thing to do would be to just close her ears and get off about her own business. No good ever came out of meddling in things that didn't concern you.

She had taken a few tentative steps in the direction of the kitchen door, when abruptly, the noise stopped.

'Don't leave me! Please!' The kitten said in a small, tear choked voice.

Mistflower almost bolted, but she made the mistake of glancing at him. What she saw caused her to stop in her tracks.

The little, black and white kitten may have stopped crying but the misery in its young face was unmistakable. Mistflower could not find it in her to abandon him.

'Well ... I ... I ... err.' Mistflower had no clue what to say. 'What ... err ... I mean ... how can I ... help you?' She finally offered.

'What are you doing out here?'

The kitten's tears flowed faster. 'I – I don't know,' he wailed. 'T-they put me in a bag and when I managed to get out, I – I didn't know where I was.' He sniffed. 'I – I've been looking … everywhere. For a long time but … I can't find my way home. And … somehow, I just ended up here. Well, not here exactly, just down the road a bit.'

'Oh dear!' She couldn't help being moved by the kitten's plight. No matter cats and mice were arch enemies; it was unthinkable someone could be so cruel to a mere baby.

By now Father Sky had draped his heavy, grey mantle of cloud across the Sun and it had grown darker. A sharp breeze had blown in from the North. Mistflower's sensitive nose twitched, even though the day had been mild, the evening wind carried a definite tang of autumn.

Her tail felt cold. She needed to gather up the wheat she had spilled onto the ground in her surprise. She needed to go home before the tawny owl began searching for his breakfast. But … there was the kitten.

She sighed glancing at the poor little creature again. No – it was no good, she simply couldn't just leave him there.

She made up her mind. Of course, her idea was plain stupid and it would serve her right if she woke up dead tomorrow morning! But her mind was made up and when her mind was made up … well … that was that!

'Come on,' she said quickly, before she could lose courage.

The kitten didn't ask any questions, simply doing as he was told. Mistflower rapidly covered the distance to the old back door with him trotting along beside her.

The door was locked of course and boarded over at the bottom where someone had once fitted a cat flap. Luckily, the boarding had come loose at one end and dropped down, quickly pulling the rusty nails free from what had already been, soft rotting wood, so that now the plank leaned drunkenly against the step.

The kitten needed no urging and before she could say a thing, he'd disappeared through the flap.

Mistflower slipped under the door. He was standing waiting for her immediately inside, and the urge to turn tail and run was almost overwhelming but when she glanced at his thin, black face with the little white bow that started either side of his nose and met beneath his chin, blossoming into a soft white bib across his chest, she lost all fear.

Why, she said to herself, he's just like any other baby that finds itself alone in the world ... lost and afraid. What kind of mouse would I be if I abandoned him now?

As if sensing some of her inner struggle, he backed away a few paces and sat down, wrapping his black tail with the white tip around his white toed paws. He sniffed. 'This is a big house,' he said, looking around the kitchen.

She was just about to tell him it wasn't any ordinary house, it was a vicarage, when the most terrible noise emerged from his stomach. Mistflower knew exactly what that loud, rumbling, grumbling sound was ... it was the sound of hunger. A frightened squeak escaped her and she felt her heart go bang-bang, with a beat that pounded in her ears.

'Oops,' he looked shamefaced. 'So-rry, I – I couldn't stop it.'

'No – *oh*!' Mistflower scampered away across the floor, to the hole in the skirting board, the kitten following in hot pursuit. She disappeared through it.

'Hey, where are you going? Don't – don't go! He pressed one eye to the mouse hole. 'I – I don't like being on my own.'

'It's all right,' Mistflower called, eying a chunk of old cheese someone had dropped in the lane a couple of days ago and she had dragged home. She had been saving it to have when all the hard work of harvesting was done; a small celebration, recalling times past. Well, better the cheese than me, she told herself and giving a great shove, pushed it out through the mouse hole.

'Here, have this.'

He stared at the lump of cheese hungrily but made no move toward it. 'Are you sure?' He asked. 'It doesn't feel right to be taking your food.'

'Oh, that's fine,' Mistflower insisted, a touch desperately. 'I've plenty of food.' Barely had she finished speaking before the cheese disappeared into the kitten's mouth and down its throat, into its belly.

Mistflower couldn't help but stare. The cheese, which would have done her for three or four meals, hadn't even been a proper mouthful for the kitten. She barely succeeded in stifling a groan. What have you got yourself into now, she asked herself.

Even if the kitten didn't kill her before morning, how on earth was she going to feed the thing? It was hard enough these days trying to feed herself and she wasn't getting any younger either. She couldn't run about all day as she had once been able to.

Remembering those days made her smile, her and Sage, young, strong, busy all the long day, working, playing together, always together. Mistflower held back a sigh; the past was a much happier place to live than the present.

She looked at the kitten again, tomorrow she would have to sort something out, but that was tomorrow. Tonight all she had to do was stay alive and The Great God would have to take care of everything else.

He had started washing himself, licking one furry paw again and again with his pink tongue before rubbing it around his ears and the top of his head. It suddenly came to her that she didn't know what to call him.

'What's your name?'

'Well,' the kitten paused. 'My mistress Sarah calls me Boots, 'cause of my white paws. But my mommy,' he paused again but not before Mistflower had heard the tears, thick in his young voice, making her own heart sore.

'My mommy calls me Silk, because she says my fur is as soft

as silk.'

'Good night, Silk', Mistflower said softly. 'Tomorrow we're going to sit down and work out what we need to do. For tonight, sleep well.'

She settled down just outside the mouse hole, telling herself if the kitten tried to attack her, she would be able to slip into her nest before any harm came to her. She slept badly; one ear listening out for any movements from the kitten, her whiskers twitching constantly and tail moving restlessly all night long.

Silk, slept soundly, his rest only disturbed by occasional dreams, when his paws would dance and his whiskers tremble and small, unhappy sounds burst from his white fur covered throat.

Each time she heard those sounds Mistflower's heart would hurt for what he had gone through. It didn't matter he was a cat, he was just a baby and no one should do bad things to babies, no matter whose babies they were.

When she awoke it was to a soft, rhythmic rumbling sound. She stretched and one paw touched something soft and silky. *Oh! Goodness!* Even before she opened her eyes, Mistflower knew it was Silk she was touching. *Oh! Goodness!* He was right on top of her! If he opened his mouth now, she would slide straight down his throat and nothing she could do to stop it.

Almost as if he could sense her fears, Silk only lay there, purring. Gradually, Mistflower relaxed and her heart stopped trying to break right through her chest. Now the pounding in her ears had quieted, she could hear another sound, the sound of an exceedingly hungry belly. Mistflower fidgeted anxiously with her whiskers. She had no more food to give him, not that he would eat anyway.

Her mind worked furiously. She had to find a way to feed him. She shuddered to think what would happen if she couldn't figure something out; either Silk would die, or he'd get so hungry he would eat her. Neither thought was good.

Suddenly she had an idea. She would ask farmer John's cows for some milk.

Silk happily followed her when she told him to. He asked no questions, nor did he mention his hunger, although his stomach growled loudly from time to time. He seemed content with nothing more than her company.

Mistflower could understand that, understand how terrible it was to be all alone with no one to care if you were laughing or crying, if you lived or died.

By the time they reached Farmer John's field the Sun was smiling down on them and shedding his warmth in all directions. They slipped under the gate and stood watching the cows, tails lazily swishing the flies away, chewing the cud in companionable silence.

Now they were here, Mistflower was a lot less certain about asking for milk. For a moment despair overwhelmed her but then Silk's belly rumbled and she knew that from somewhere she was going to have to find the courage to do this thing, because yesterday she had made Silk her responsibility and the Great God would surely hold her to task if she did any less than her best now.

Reluctantly, she started forward, with Silk staying tight by her side. They edged slowly closer and closer, Mistflower growing increasingly nervous with each step, until eventually, they could hear the sighing sounds of warm breath being exhaled, the steady chomp of jaws chewing cud and the soft thud of hooves on the earth as cows moved from one patch of the sweet and tender, green grass to another.

Mistflower knew she had to act straight away because if she gave herself the time, she would just turn tail and sprint for home. She scampered around to the head of the nearest cow.

'Excuse me,' she squeaked.

Startled, the cow lifted her head and danced back a few steps before regaining her calm. She fixed Mistflower with a suspicious stare.

'I'm so sorry to interrupt your breakfast,' Mistflower rushed on. 'I – I found a kitten, he – someone put him in a bag and dropped him in the lane and well, he's hungry and I've no more food to give him and … I was just wondering … if you could spare him a little milk.'

The cow glared at her.

'Milk! You want *me* to give my lovely, creamy milk to some scruffy little kitten?' She mooed loudly. 'And … and you … you're … a *rodent*, how dare you come here making demands of *me!*

'Well,' Mistflower squeaked. 'There's no need for name calling. He's just a baby and he's all alone and … he, he wouldn't need very much really,' she finished humbly.

'You'd both better get out of my field before I run you out,' the big, tan coloured cow said, bringing her head to within a hair's breadth of Mistflower's whiskers.

Mistflower inched carefully backward, her eyes never leaving the cow for a second. The little mouse knew danger when it stared her in the face. Her heart thud-thudded in her chest. She tensed, waiting for a huge hoof to come crashing down on her.

True Friends

'Just a minute, Caramel.'

Another light cream, coloured cow stopped chewing and stepped up alongside. Mistflower spotted a calf pressed close to her; its large liquid brown eyes were fixed on Silk.

'If someone took my little Lilac and abandoned her somewhere, I'd call on the Great God to send someone to help her and not let her be alone and afraid. This kitten's mother might also have asked The Great God for the same help and this little mouse might be The Great God's answer to a desperate mother's prayer.'

Mistflower watched as the cow's great, long tongue appeared and she gave Lilac a couple of affectionate licks before turning back to Mistflower.

'I'll help you,' she said, ignoring the disgusted lowing of Caramel. 'Come with me.' With that she started across the field, in the direction of the barn.

22

'Shut it, Caramel,' she threw back over her shoulder. 'It's not *your* field. We all live here. You don't own it and as far as I remember, nobody put you in charge.'

She gazed down at them. 'By the way, my name's Lavender.' Mistflower quickly introduced herself and Silk.

'Well, Silk,' Lavender said. 'You're a very lucky kitten to find such a friend, and you, Mistflower, are a very brave and good little mouse.'

She ran her glance over them both again. 'And there's no denying it,' she laughed warmly, 'you do make a very odd couple.'

Lavender led them over to the barn.

'After Farmer John's wife has milked us, she takes the buckets and empties them but there's always plenty of milk left in the bottom.' She nudged Silk gently with her nose. 'If you're really lucky, there might be a broken egg to be had from one of the hens as well or perhaps even a really large one from Sedgehop, the duck.'

There were four buckets in all. Standing in a neat row along one side of the barn and while Silk was busy licking them spotlessly clean, Lavender found him a cracked duck egg. They watched as he carefully mopped up every last morsel of the rich egg from the shell.

'I'll never be able to thank you enough.' Mistflower gave Lavender a long, grateful look. 'I don't know what I would've done without your help.'

'Don't you worry now,' Lavender told her. There's always plenty of food around a farmhouse.' She glanced at Silk who was contentedly washing his whiskers. He burped delicately and giggled shyly.

Lilac, who hadn't taken her eyes of Silk since first meeting him, giggled back. 'Don't worry,' she said. 'Mum and I know what it's like to be a bit windy, don't we mum?' She giggled again.

'Look,' Lavender said, 'you must be starving yourself.'

Mistflower had to admit she was pretty hungry. With all the fuss of getting Silk fed, she hadn't eaten a thing since the previous evening.

'Why don't you leave him here? He'll be fine with Lilac and I'll keep an eye on them. You go and get yourself fed and don't you fret. I won't let anything happen to him.'

Mistflower threw Lavender another grateful glance, 'You're so kind, Lavender,' she said. 'And to one such as me, a despised mouse! I – I'll never forget what you've done for me.'

'Ooh – go on, away with you! What I've done is nothing compared with what you're doing.' Lavender tossed her head. 'You're a very, very good creature, Mistflower.

'Now, if you take yourself off around to that side of the barn there,' Lavender angled her head left, 'you'll see a mound of old corn stalks and I'm betting that amongst all those stalks there'll be enough nibletts for a little mouse to make herself a good breakfast on.'

At that moment Mistflower wanted nothing more than to run up Lavender's leg, onto her big, broad shoulder, and plant a little mouse kiss on the fur covering her beautiful head.

Instead she stood there, wondering how she would ever be able to repay this wonderful, generous hearted, new friend. But before she could find the words to express how she felt, Lavender lowered her head again, giving her a gentle push.

'Go on with you, go and get some food inside you before you die of hunger.' Then she was gone, walking sedately away toward the open barn door.

Lavender was as good as her word and soon Mistflower was munching blissfully on the flavour packed, yellow buds. Finally, her hunger satisfied, she sat on top of the pile and carefully washed her face and groomed her whiskers, until she was sure not a speck, not a crumb of corn remained.

The Sun sent his long rays of comfortable warmth down onto

her and Mistflower would have liked nothing more than to find a quiet spot in the hedgerows and settle down for a little snooze before completing the journey back to her nest.

Sadly, that would have to wait for another day. She had imposed on Lavender for long enough. She would have to go and collect Silk before he outstayed his welcome. Quickly, she ran down the side of the heap and scurried across the grass and into the barn.

It was cool inside and the light was dimmer but Mistflower could see Lavender, standing patiently in one corner. A little to the side, Lilac was lying, her front and back legs folded under her. For a moment she didn't see him, but then as her eyes adjusted better, Mistflower could see Silk's body curled under Lilac's chin.

As soon as he saw her, he gently drew himself out from under Lilac's head and padded softly over to where she waited.

'You came back,' he said. His green eyes fixed on her and very slowly and carefully he stuck out his tongue and gave her a lick that started at the top of her head and went all the way down her back to her tail.

'Thank you. Thank you for coming back.'

His lick lifted Mistflower clean off her paws. Lavender chuckled. 'Careful, son, or you'll wear all the fur off her head.'

'Well,' Mistflower squeaked, a little breathless still. 'We'd better get out of your way then.' She found her voice suddenly gruff with tears and snuffled and sneezed to clear them away. 'I can't thank you enough for all your help.'

'Oh – don't start all that now,' Lavender swished her tail lazily. 'Bring him back again later, around tea time. After Miss Lucy, Farmer John's daughter, has milked us again – don't leave it too long mind, or the Missus 'ull have washed the pails and all the milk 'ull be gone.'

As they made their way back up the lane, Mistflower knew she had made a good and firm friend in Lavender and she was filled with a huge relief. Everything was so much easier when you were not all alone.

Their new friend didn't let them down and when they returned later in the day, Silk made short work of cleaning up the foamy, creamy milk, while Mistflower returned to the heap of cornstalks.

That night, as she settled down to sleep, Mistflower, though still keeping a watchful eye out for any change in Silk's behaviour, realised she was happier than she had been in a long, long time.

Strange Times

As the days stretched out, they fell into a routine. In the morning they would visit with Lavender and Lilac. Silk would breakfast on lovely fresh milk, while Mistflower searched out any scraps Lavender directed her to. They'd spend the rest of the day looking for anything else they could find.

Sometimes people would drop the remains of sandwiches with cheese or, if they were really lucky, some meat in them. Mistflower would always leave those to Silk. Even with Lavender helping, Silk was still painfully thin, she could count all of his ribs, and she constantly worried about getting him enough food.

Once, they had been lucky enough to find a bun with an almost untouched flat, round of meat in it, with cheese stuck to it. Mistflower was sure, as long as she lived, she would never forget the look of perfect happiness on Silk's face as he steadily chomped his way through the bun, filled with delightfully smelling cheese and meat, until the very last bite disappeared down his throat and into his belly.

How she would like to put that same look on his face every day. Mistflower gave herself a shake, she did the best she could and even The Great God didn't ask a creature for more than that.

Strange as it seemed, a cat and a mouse living in harmony, Mistflower knew she had done the right thing that first day in not running away. She was even getting used to waking up between Silk's paws every morning, she realised with some amusement.

She remembered asking The Great God to take away her burden of loneliness and understood that she had been answered. Perhaps not in the way she, in her wildest dreams, might have imagined. But that she had been answered was beyond doubt.

She twitched her nose, tasting the air. The days were beginning to draw in and though she had put by enough food for herself, she knew when winter arrived, it would be harder than ever to keep Silk fed. She sighed. No point nibbling on that one, she told herself. She would have to leave that to a power greater than hers.

She glanced over at Silk, who was lying in the last rays of the Sun, lazily washing his paws and rolling onto his back to get at his, soft, white underbelly. She had been about to call to him but she stopped, struck afresh, as she had been so many times when she looked at him, by how large a place in her heart he had made his.

His sixth sense told Silk he was being watched, he flipped over onto his side and fixed her with his beautiful green eyes.

'Come on then,' Mistflower squeaked. 'It's time we visited Lavender and Lilac. We'd better be quick too, or the pails will be washed and your belly will be rumbling louder than ever tonight.'

Silk sprang to his feet, a wide grin on his furry face. 'I love going there,' he meowed. 'I like playing with Lilac.'

'Hello, you two.' Lavender was waiting for them and as soon as she heard her mother, Lilac rushed around from the other side of the stall, where she had been visiting with Larkspur, the old plough horse. She trotted over to Silk, 'Oh – good, you're here, we can play now.'

'Let him eat first, Lilac.' Lavender butted her calf affectionately. 'He won't have much energy to play if you don't let him get his food.'

'Sorry, Mum.' Lilac hung her head, shamefaced

Lavender planted a kiss on Lilac's muzzle. She glanced at Silk, who thinking his friend Lilac was in trouble, had been hopping nervously from one paw to another. Seeing all was well, he wound his body around Lavender's front hock, purring loudly.

Lavender chuckled. 'Go on, go and clean out those buckets 'afore the Missus does.'

Silk had barely settled to lapping up the milk when a shadow fell across the open barn door.

'Well … now I've lived to see it all.'

Mistflower froze as Storm, the sheepdog, slipped inside the barn. All her instincts screamed, *RUN*, dogs could be as bad as cats for catching mice. Then a movement in the corner of her eye stole her attention and she turned her head to see Silk's milk smeared mouth appear above the rim of a bucket and knew she could not run and save herself if it meant abandoning Silk.

She glanced around wildly, searching for an opening, somewhere to hide for them both. But even as she looked she knew it would be impossible. There were plenty of places where a small mouse could lose herself, perhaps even a skinny kitten but even if she could make Silk understand what she wanted him to do, by the time he did, it would already be too late and the dog would be upon them.

'Caramel's been going on about it for days.' Storm's voice was filled with wonder. 'I thought she was joking, having me on. But by jingo, she was telling me right all along.'

Fear had Mistflower in its iron grip. It tightened her chest so that her whole rib cage heaved with the effort of drawing a breath. Her heart pounded in her ears, making it hard to form an idea. She could see Silk's green eyes fixed trustingly on her.

Finding The Truth

So — Caramel had betrayed them. She should've known, Mistflower thought sickly. She should've seen it coming and because she'd been too stupid to realise, she'd placed Silk in grave danger.

'Storm ...' Lavender stepped forward, placing herself between Storm and Silk. 'Look, I know we should've discussed it with you. It's your farmyard, after all but—'

'A *mouse* and a kitten!' Storm growled, ignoring Lavender. He glanced from Mistflower to Silk. 'Well, whoever would? I'm seeing it with my own eyes and I still can't believe it.'

She would run, Mistflower decided. At the last moment, just as Storm went for Silk, she would run right across his path and distract him. With The Great God's help, perhaps she could buy Silk enough time to get away. It was all she had left to do.

Mistflower readied herself for the last chase of her life.

At that instant Storm dropped to his haunches, swinging his

head back toward her. 'Well, Mistress Mouse,' he said. 'There's only one thing left for any self-respecting sheep dog to do.'

'Storm!' Lavender begged.

'No – Mummy! No!' Lilac cried.

Mistflower gathered herself.

'As I was saying,' Storm continued. 'There's only one thing any self-respecting sheep dog can do in such unique circumstances as these.' He paused, his eyes sweeping over the small assembly. 'From now on, once a day – you.' His gaze locked on Silk. 'What's your name, youngling?'

Silk, bewildered, sensing something badly amiss and afraid of Storm but not really understanding what was happening, stammered. 'S-s-silk … Sir.'

'Silk. Well … Silk. From now on, once a day, you'll come up to the farm house and I'll see to it you get some meat inside that scrawny carcass. Understand?'

'*No!*'

No one had noticed Caramel enter the barn.

'You – you can't do this to me! What kind of sheep dog are you anyway? Your barn's infested with vermin and *you* want to help feed them?'

Storm growled low in his throat. 'Watch your tongue, Caramel.' He warned.

'Don't you threaten me, you absurd little hound.'

The next second Caramel mooed in pain as Storm lunged forward, nipping at her ankles. Lifting her tail, she ran from the barn, lowing furiously.

'T-thank you … so very, very, much, from both of us.' Mistflower was shaking. It was all she could do to stay on her feet but she thanked Storm and The Great God, both, for this unbelievable, incredible, kindness.

'Oh – it's the least I can do.' Storm ducked his head, embarrassed.

'You're a fine sheep dog, Storm.' Lavender told him, planting a kiss on his muzzle. 'And I'm proud to call you my friend.'

Word spread like mould on cheese after that. Very soon every animal for miles around seemed to know about Mistflower and Silk. Some of the animals even helped. Hurricane, the Hawk, often came by with scraps of meat for Silk. Somehow he had discovered Mistflower liked chocolate and sometimes there would be a piece of that for her, along with the meat for Silk.

Storm kept to his promise also. Every morning, soon after the Farmer's wife put out the leftovers from the previous evening's meal, Silk would venture up to the house and eat his fill while Storm looked on peacefully.

The first day, Mistflower was so afraid they almost hadn't gone but Lavender insisted they must.

'You can't not go,' Lavender said, flicking her tail, agitated. 'Storm would be hurt – it's so rude when he's offered his help.'

Mistflower knew Lavender was right, but her being right didn't take the fear away.

'Trust him,' Lavender pressed. 'It'll all be okay, you'll see. Storm'll make sure no harm comes to either of you at his bowl. Besides, winter's on its way and it'll be harder than ever for you to keep Silk fed.'

Mistflower was no longer afraid of Storm and she was much relieved to see Silk filling out and growing into a big, beautiful animal. For just the tiniest moment she acknowledged the strangeness of a mouse finding pleasure in the well-being of a cat. Then she dismissed the thought. Silk had brought love and warmth and companionship into her life again.

Not only was Silk himself a constant joy, through him she had found many new friends she would otherwise never have met. For the thousandth time she thanked The Great God for her wonderful and wise friend, Lavender. Without her, Mistflower knew things would have been so much harder.

* * *

Mistflower glanced around the vicarage garden. The Sun was climbing down the sky and there was no sign of Silk. Since he had been eating better, he had more energy and more natural curiosity. Mistflower accepted his new found independence as she had accepted her own children's. But she had never known him be this late and she couldn't help worrying. He was still only a very young cat, after all.

Shadows stretched ever lengthening fingers across the ground as Mistflower waited, filled with a growing dread. Several times, she ventured into the lane but there was no sign of him and after a while, afraid that Ghost or the tawny owl would be out searching for their breakfast, Mistflower hurried back to the safety of the overgrown garden.

Finally, as Night began to unfold her shawl across Father Sky, she spied him heading home. He was all the way across the garden but Mistflower could immediately see something was badly wrong. Her heart leapt up into her mouth. He was moving so slowly ... and ... clumsily ... almost dragging himself along.

Then her heart almost stopped completely because as Mistress Moon peeked out from behind a cloud, Mistflower saw it wasn't Silk there was something wrong with, it was Blackthorn!

Silk had the blackbird in his mouth and the poor things wings were dragging between his front paws, forcing Silk to waddle.

A terrible pain crashed down on her as she stood there, realizing that the kitten she had loved with all her heart was gone. In his place was what, after all, he'd really been all along; the mouse's arch enemy ... a cat. She should run ... now, she thought dully, while she still had a chance, before Silk killed her too. But there was a crushing heaviness in her limbs and she just could not make herself move.

Silk was almost upon her now, dragging the unmoving form of Blackthorn and still her legs refused to co-operate.

He reached her, dropping the blackbird on the ground in front of her. 'Pfffwwwttt.' He spat feathers.

Mistflower stared blankly as he used his paws to dislodge another downy feather. How could this be, she asked herself? How could that frightened little kitten they had all given so much too, turn into this ... this ... unfeeling monster!

'Help me!'

Help him? Mistflower tried hard to shake off the fog that had fallen upon her. What did he want her to do? Did he want her to help him eat poor Blackthorn? What did this terrible creature want from her now?

'He's hurt. We've got to help him, Mistflower! I didn't know what to do. And I couldn't just leave him, alone and sick. So ... I brought him home.' Silk trailed off uncertainly.

Suddenly, the daze lifted and clarity came back to her thoughts. Silk hadn't killed Blackthorn. He wasn't a monster at all. He was just trying to help the injured bird. She was overcome by shame. How quickly she had judged him. How wrong she had been.

'I did the right thing, didn't I? You can help him, can't you?'

Mistflower stared at Silk's worried face. After a moment, she nodded. 'Yes, Silk. You did the right thing. Now,' she ran over to Blackthorn. 'Let me take a look.'

She could see straight away the bird was in a bad way. His eyes had the glassy look of death and he was barely breathing.

An icy wind had blown in, cutting the temperature. Mistflower knew cold on top of shock would be the end of Blackthorn.

'We need to get him warm,' she told Silk. 'Let's get him inside.'

Mistflower ran ahead as Silk struggled to get Blackthorn through the cat flap.

She searched frantically for something out of which she could make some kind of nest for the bird. Finding an old newspaper she set about tearing it into strips, piling the strips on top of each other and scratching about until she had formed a small well.

'Lay him on here,' she instructed.

Silk carefully laid Blackthorn down on the nest. 'I'll stay beside him and keep him warm,' he told her.

'That's a really good idea, Silk. I'll lie on the other side of him too, that way he'll be even warmer.'

Mistflower knew it was going to be touch and go. If Blackthorn survived until morning it would be a miracle. Well, they would just have to do what they could and leave the rest up to The Great God.'

'D'you know what happened?'

'No.' Silk carefully fitted himself around Blackthorn. 'I just found him on the ground.'

'Hmm. Did you notice any marks on him? Bites or scratches?'

'No. I looked but I couldn't see anything. No blood, nothing.'

Mistflower was puzzled. What could have happened to Blackthorn? With no tell tale marks and nothing else to go on it was a complete mystery and although Blackthorn's beak opened and closed he seemed unable to speak. Ah well, all that could wait. What they had to concentrate on now was keeping the blackbird alive until morning.

With Silk and herself on either side, Blackthorn began to warm up a little. Mistflower could tell his breathing was better. Even so, it was going to be a long night for all of them.

Towards dawn, Blackthorn seemed to revive. 'Water,' he croaked. 'Water.'

Mistflower slipped outside and returned, carefully dragging a leaf. It had rained throughout the night and the leaf, which was a nice curvy one, had held onto its raindrops.

The blackbird buried his beak in the wet leaf. 'More,' he looked at Mistflower. 'More.'

Silk was out of the cat flap before she could even move. A few minutes later he returned dragging an old and battered paper tub, the sort humans spooned white, creamy, icy sludge from. It was full of clean, fresh rainwater.

Blackthorn drank his fill. 'Thank you,' he said finally. He looked at Silk. 'I owe you my life, young man. I wouldn't have survived without you,' he glanced at Mistflower, 'both.'

He struggled to his feet, shaking out his wings. Wincing in pain, he hopped a few steps. 'Not too bad,' he muttered. Then, in a firmer voice, 'It'll do.'

'What happened to you, Blackthorn?' Mistflower asked. 'We couldn't find a mark on you.'

'Oh there's a mark all right. Just not the kind of mark you'd have been looking for.' Blackthorn spread his wings. 'See?' He said, pointing with his beak.

Right at the edge of his left wing, just below where the flight feathers sprouted, Mistflower spotted a strange charred area, as if the feathers there and the flesh beneath had been burned.

She stared hard at the place. What kind of animal could have done this to the blackbird?

'The thing that did this to me is a huge snake,' Blackthorn told her. 'It's very long and thin and its skin is hard and cold. It makes a noise, a low hum and its home is in the sky, at the top of a tall pole. Its bite is terrible indeed, as soon as it touches you, it feels as if your whole body is being torn apart.

'Aaaeeehh!' Mistflower was filled with fear at the idea of such a terrible creature.

'I'd seen what happened to other birds that were bitten and I knew to keep away from it but I was running from the Falcon and … next thing I knew, I was on the ground, thrashing about in agony, unable to defend myself and sure I was looking my last upon the Earth.' He laughed. 'Especially when I saw a cat appear and start sniffing at me. It was only when he dropped me at your feet that I recognised who he was.'

'You know about us?' Mistflower was astonished. She hadn't realised just how far their story had spread.

'Oh yes, I'd heard. I hadn't believed it mind.' He cocked his head from side to side, glancing from Mistflower to Silk. 'I certainly believe it now – and thank The Great God for you both. I owe you a debt,' he said, hopping toward the kitchen door. 'As does the rest of the blackbird clan.' He turned toward them again. 'If you're ever in need, just find a blackbird. Now, if you'd kindly show me how to get out of this room, I'll be on my way. My wife will be worrying.'

'Oh – yes, of course! Actually, now it came to it, Mistflower wasn't at all sure how Blackthorn would get out. She eyed Silk. Somehow, she didn't think Blackthorn would be too happy for the feel of Silk's teeth again.

Silk came to the rescue. 'You'll have to go out through the flap', he explained. I'll push it up with my nose and you'll have to fly through.'

Luckily, the old boarding had completely dropped away by now and the flap pushed up easily, leaving enough space for Blackthorn to escape.

Mistflower ran under the door. 'Wait,' she called. 'I've some bread and cheese. You should eat before you go, get your strength up. You've been through a terrible ordeal.'

'I'll eat as I go,' Blackthorn sang, lifting up into the air.

Mistflower and Silk gazed after him until he was completely out of sight. 'I hope he gets home safe,' Silk said.

Mistflower sighed, 'So do I,' she told him. 'So do I.'

She had often envied the birds their freedom of the air. Now she realised their lives were just as fraught with danger as her own.

* * *

Late that afternoon winter fully arrived with a rush and Father Snow covered the Earth with his soft, white blanket. Mistflower gazed up at the Morning Star, content. With the help of their friends they would get through the cold spell.

In only a short space of time things had gone from her struggling to get Silk fed, to Silk often being the one bringing her titbits and the chocolate and peanut butter she'd found scouting around the waste at the farm had provided her with more than her share of pleasure.

Suddenly she was aware of a pale, silent and deadly shape, silhouetted against the dark sky. Frozen, Mistflower could only stare as the barn owl ghosted down towards her.

She had grown careless in her old age. Now she would surely pay!

'Evening, Mistress Mouse.'

'E-evening.' Mistflower willed herself to breath as the owl glided away just as Silk appeared from around the side of the vicarage.

'You'll never believe what just happened,' she squeaked, still trying to steady her breathing. 'G-Ghost just flew by and s-said g-good evening. I thought I was finished for sure but he – he didn't even try to catch me.'

Silk yawned. 'Course not.'

'W-what d'you mean – course not?'

'Oh! I forgot.'

'Forgot what?'

'I forgot to tell you – Storm said Ghost's let all the creatures know you're under his protection and no one's to harm you or they'll have to answer to him.'

'He said …' Mistflower trailed off in astonishment.

'Well, everyone thinks you're really brave.' Silk yawned again.

'Brave? Me?'

'Yep.' Silk scratched behind his ear. 'I don't really understand it either,' he said, seeing her puzzlement. 'I mean, it's not like I'd ever hurt you or anything.'

Mistflower remembered her fear the evening they'd first met. How she'd thought Silk would want to chase her until she was too exhausted to run anymore and then bite her head off.

'No,' she said, wryly. 'It's not as if cats and mice aren't usually the best of friends.'

'Exac-tly.' Silk stared at her a moment. 'W-well, I 'pose you might've been scared,' he said. 'But I'd never have hurt you. I'm not that kind of cat.'

'No,' Mistflower said, keeping her voice gentle. 'I know that now, Silk, and I can't tell you how happy having you here's made me.'

Silk looked bashful. 'I – I've never really thanked you – for all you've done for me. I – I don't know what I would've done without you. Thank you, Mistflower. With all my heart – thank you.'

'Come on,' Mistflower said, scampering up Silk's leg, along his back, onto his head and placing a little mouse kiss on the tip of his black nose. 'Let's get inside quick, in case that lad Frost nips along and freezes your paws to the ground when you're not looking.'

Nestled next to Silk's warm body, Mistflower fell asleep in a moment.

The next time she opened her eyes it was already morning and Silk was gone. Mistflower wasn't worried, Silk often went out during the night. She curled herself into a tighter ball, resisting the cold and let herself drift.

She was still drifting when she heard the cat flap but Silk's frightened meow brought her eyes open, her mind wide awake and her body readied for flight.

Bad Things

'What is it, Silk?'

'Big … huge creatures! Horrible, glaring eyes and … humans riding them.'

'What on Earth are you saying, Silk? What … creatures? Where?'

'*Here*! They're *here*, Mistflower! They're knocking down the wall! *Now*! And coming here!'

Now she was fully awake, Mistflower realised she could hear them; a low, threatening mutter and growl and a dull repeating thud that shook the ground, and carried right into the house.

She had to find out what was going on! Swiftly, she climbed the musty curtains and ran along the sill until she found a small space clear of frosty patterns. What she saw chilled her more than any wind or snow ever could.

Silk was right. The creatures were coming into their garden. Even as she watched, one of them, a big, bright yellow thing, hit the wall and as it backed away, Mistflower saw the wall buckle and a shower of bricks fell into the garden as a hole appeared.

The creature reared up, smashing into the wall again and this time part of the wall disappeared, leaving a pile of rubble in its place.

Silk had leapt up beside her and together, in stunned silence, they watched as the things poured onto their land. They watched horrified as the crab apple tree, which had spread its boughs to the birds and fed both them and church men alike, was torn up by its roots and toppled onto its side. They watched as the sylph, the tree spirit, who had resided so long within it, sobbed wretchedly, huddled against its grainy bark.

Mistflower turned away, she could watch no more.

'What – what will we do, Mistflower?'

Mistflower tried not to look as frightened as she felt.

'What can we do, Silk, against creatures such as that?' She forced her voice to a calmness she couldn't feel. 'All might yet be well. We don't know what they intend. They might just want the garden,' she said, trying to dispel his fears.

The things had come to a halt and Mistflower and Silk could hear the men driving them calling to each other. Their sensitive ears could make out the words but they couldn't understand them. They were talking about sewers and foundations and cables, none of the words made sense to Mistflower or Silk.

All morning they hid inside, anxiously waiting to see what would happen. Men tramped around the garden and unrolled papers, which they examined intently. Several times they pointed at the vicarage. They unloaded stuff from the monstrous creatures but Mistflower and Silk had never seen such items before and had no idea what they were or what purpose they might serve.

Around midday all the men disappeared and it wasn't long after that when they heard Storm barking by the kitchen door.

'You've got to get out!' Storm said, the instant he saw them.

'But . . .'

'No buts, Mistflower. You have to leave, now! They're demolishing the vicarage. I heard Master and Missus talking about it over breakfast.

'When Silk didn't show up for his food, I knew you must be trapped inside. So I waited until the men had gone and came straight here to warn you.'

'But how will we get past those creatures?' Mistflower glanced toward where the things stood idle. 'Won't they attack us?'

'No.' Storm wagged his tail encouragingly. 'Those things aren't alive, Mistflower. They're machines, like Master's tractor or his car.

'Men have to make the machines do what they want them to. Without the men you can do anything you like and the machine won't even move. Look, I'll show you.'

Storm ran over to the bright yellow monster that had smashed down the garden wall. He lifted his leg and watered the side of it. 'See?' He called running back to them. 'You're quite safe. As long as we're gone before the men get back.'

'I can't leave, Storm.' Mistflower's voice shook. She felt as if her heart would break. 'It's my home.

'Why do they want to take my home away from me? What harm have I or any of my family ever done to any of them? All our kind has ever done is tidy up the mess men leave behind them.'

Storm looked sad. 'Men just don't think about anyone but themselves. If another creature gets in their way, well, they just … get rid of them.'

Mistflower lifted wide, frightened eyes to him. 'But where will we go? It's winter and all my food … we … we can't survive outside in this weather.'

'You won't have to.' Storm grinned. 'You're coming with me, to the barn. That's your new home now.'

'But …'

'It's all right, Mistflower. It's what we want.' He glanced away.

'We – we've grown quite fond of you both.

'As for food, you won't go short with us. So stop your worrying, mouse, and hurry up and get going before the men come back.'

Mistflower gazed at the house where she had spent most of her life. So many memories! Well, she told herself, no one could take those away from her. She would carry those with her forever.

'Mistflower, can we go now!' Silk begged. 'I don't want those men coming back while we're still here. T-they might tie me up in a bag.'

'Yes, okay. Let's go.'

It's not the end of the world, she thought. At least we've got somewhere to go to.

Then why did it feel as if it was? Why was it she just wanted to lay down and go to sleep and never wake up again?

Don't be stupid, she told herself, angrily. You've got Silk to look out for. He needs you. So just you stop feeling sorry for yourself.

Part of it, she knew, was that no matter what Storm had said, Mistflower knew at least one resident of the barn would be a lot more than just unhappy to see them moving in.

After Storm chasing her out of the barn, the first day they'd met him, Caramel would be absolutely furious about having them both living on her territory.

* * *

The snow made it heavy going for a little mouse and Mistflower was quickly wet and chilled to the bone and very soon she was exhausted.

Silk, who had been keeping a careful eye on her, lowered his head to the ground. 'Jump up,' he said. 'You'll be nice and dry and out of the wind in my fur.'

Gratefully, Mistflower climbed aboard and burrowed down in

his thick, black fur.

They've taken our house, Sage, she thought. It was the same thought she'd had in her head since they had set out. She felt she must surely die of grief and yet, nestled in the warmth of Silk's body heat, she willed herself to heal. She had a responsibility to Silk. She didn't want to leave him on his own, not just yet. He was still just a youngling after all.

He would need someone to watch his back, particularly with Caramel around.

'S-Storm?' Silk was keeping his voice low, but Mistflower still heard him.

'Yes, Silk,' Storm said kindly.

'I – I know you said everyone wants us to live in the barn … but … what about Caramel? Does she want us to live there too?'

'Don't you worry about Caramel, youngling. I've had a word with her and you won't be having any trouble there.'

'Oh – t-thank you, Storm.'

Mistflower thought Silk sounded as miserable and unsure of everything as she was. She made up her mind to pull herself together. She was not going to leave him to struggle with all this without any support from her.

'Just think, Silk,' she said. 'You won't have to go up to the farm in this cold anymore – and you can play with Lilac all day long, if you want to.'

'That's right. Yes,' Silk said, brightening up a little. 'It's all going to be fine, isn't it Mistflower?'

'Of course it is!' She told him firmly. 'We're so lucky, you and I – to have such wonderful friends.' That part, at least, was absolutely true.

* * *

'They're coming,' Lilac mooed, excited. She had been on watch since Storm had left. 'I can see them. They're all right!' She dashed into the snow to meet the little party.

'Silk! You're going to live with us! In the barn.'

Silk, forgetting Mistflower was still on his neck, sprang forward. 'I know.'

'Careful!' Mistflower warned, running quickly down his leg and onto the ground.

'Oops! Sorry.' He giggled, the warm welcome from his good friend immediately lifting his spirits.

Mistflower was glad to see Silk happier. She glanced around, searching for Caramel but she was nowhere in sight. That troubled Mistflower more than if Caramel had just openly protested about them. She began to wonder what the big, tan coloured cow might be plotting. Well, nothing they could do about it until it happened. She might as well rest and enjoy what she could until then.

One by one the animals gathered round to welcome them and by the end of the day Silk already seemed to have settled in. Mistflower knew it was going to take her a lot longer to come to terms with things. Still, she didn't want to spoil Silk's fun so she tried her best to look happy. She didn't have to try to look grateful – she was. Without their friends, she would most likely already be dead and Silk would probably have been in serious trouble and on his way to joining her.

At some point during the evening, Caramel came in from the fields and it seemed whatever Storm had said to her had worked because she joined in with the others in welcoming the two of them. Time would tell, Mistflower thought. Just because Caramel said the words, didn't mean she meant them. Mistflower was going to keep a watchful eye on that one, until she could be sure, one way or the other.

It snowed for days, huge, white flakes, no two exactly the same pattern, falling out of a heavy grey sky and by the time it stopped, Mistflower couldn't imagine living anywhere else ever again. It was strange, how what could seem like the very worst thing that could happen to a body, could turn out to be the very best.

She'd put a brave face on things for the sake of Silk but when she lost her home she'd thought it would be the end of her. Yet, here she was, living in the barn and loving every moment.

The vicarage had been damp and cold and the air inside had been stale, even at the height of summer, and before Silk had come it had also been very quiet, too quiet in fact.

The barn was busy and friendly and the air, while it smelled of animals, was fresh and clean. Due to all the warm bodies, and on the coldest of nights, Farmer John's heaters, it was warm even in the dead of winter.

Mistflower glanced at the high, small clouds and decided the snow was behind them for this season. Each day, she had watched it melt further and further into Mother Earth and finally it had all but gone, leaving only patches spread here and there.

A watery Sun shone down from an icy blue sky and Mistflower decided it was time to go outside and forage for some food. She knew neither she, nor Silk would ever be allowed to go hungry. Their new friends were far too kind for that and there was always food around but Mistflower didn't want to feel herself to be a burden, besides, she wouldn't go far and the walk would do her good.

She set off down the path toward the farmhouse. A few days ago she wouldn't have believed anyone who had tried to tell her she would ever feel this good again. She thanked The Great God for her and Silk's good fortune. Even Caramel, Mistflower realised, had made them welcome. Perhaps she had been wrong to be suspicious of her. Perhaps Caramel truly had changed.

All around her was silence and the beauty of the land. Most of the creatures she would normally have seen were safe in their nests and burrows.

Only the birds who had stayed, to brave the cold, still flew the skies.

A long way down, near the pond, she could see Blackthorn. She remembered the day Silk had struggled home with the injured bird and tried not to think too long about how she had wrongly judged him that day. They had seen Blackthorn and his family often since then. He had brought his wife and his children to meet them and they had thanked them both for saving his life. After that, whenever Blackthorn had spotted something either she or Silk would like he had made it a point to call and tell them.

Mistflower glanced back toward the barn, she had left Silk asleep. Perhaps she should wait until he woke up? Now you're just being silly, she told herself. What could happen to Silk in the barn? Where could he possibly be safer? Besides, she wouldn't be long, likely Silk would still be sleeping when she got back.

Betrayal

Caramel waited until she saw Mistflower round the side of the farmhouse before moving out from behind the silo. She couldn't believe her luck! She had only come back because she was so thoroughly sick and tired of choking back her anger at the rodent and that flea-bitten moggy moving into the barn and pretending she was fine with it. And lookie here, the rotten rodent had gone off and left flea-bag on its own.

She peered around carefully – just as she'd thought. The first reasonable day and everyone had abandoned the barn for a splash of winter Sun outside. Caramel glanced over her broad shoulder, searching this way and that. No one was in sight. But she would have to hurry. Who knew how long she would have before someone got cold hooves and came running back. She took a deep breath, filling her lungs up with air and ... 'MOOOOO!'

Silk came awake instantly. Even through layers of sleep the urgency of the sound had drilled into him. He sprang to his feet, glancing around wildly. The barn was empty, except for Caramel.

Suddenly Silk was afraid. What was the matter with her? Why was she making that noise? The fact he was alone with her made him very nervous. He hadn't forgotten the way she'd behaved toward him and Mistflower in the beginning. Then he recognised

49

that if she had meant to attack him, she would already have struck and he calmed down a little. Still, something was very wrong here; he could feel it in his whiskers.

'W-what's the matter, Caramel?'

'It's Mistflower.'

'Mistflower?' Dread shot through Silk like an arrow. He paused, afraid for a moment to go on, to ask the question. But then he realised he was wasting time.

'What's wrong with Mistflower? Where is she?'

'Come on,' Caramel said. 'I'll show you.' She set off down the farmyard path at a fast trot. 'Quick! She called over her shoulder. 'There's not much time.'

He tore after her. 'Where are we going?'

'No time to explain.' Caramel picked up her pace until Silk was running flat out to keep up.

She slowed as they reached the pond. 'There,' she angled her head at the small wooded area that lay beyond the frozen water. 'Mistflower's trapped in there. You've got to hurry. You'll have to cut across the pond. It'll take too long to go around.'

Silk didn't hesitate. He started across. His claws couldn't get any grip on the slippery surface. His legs kept going out from under him, sprawling him onto the ice banging his chin, but he kept going.

He glanced back once, Caramel had disappeared but he couldn't worry himself about that now. His best friend was in trouble and he had to get to her as quickly as he possibly could.

He was almost half way when he heard the sharp sound of ice cracking and a jagged line of water, black against the frozen surface, appeared under his paws.

* * *

Mistflower had been hoping to find one of her favourite foods, a crust with some peanut butter or a piece of chocolate, but although she had seen a discarded peanut butter jar wedged into an overflowing bin, the top of the jar was firmly in place and there was no way for a mouse to get at the tempting smears of the rich butter inside. She had settled instead for the crumbs of a chocolate cake in its paper wrapper and although it wasn't quite as good as a piece of chocolate she had made herself a good breakfast of it.

She came around the side of the barn and stopped. The Sun had climbed high in the sky in the time she had been away. The farmstead was built on a slight hill and below her the fields spread out like a lovely patchwork of different hued greens and yellows, from the deepest sea green to a light mustard colour.

Mistflower knew what a patchwork was because she had seen one on the vicar's bed and heard the housekeeper talk about it but she had never been near the sea. Even so, something within her, some place deep inside, knew exactly what the sea was and all of its moods.

She took a long hungry look, marvelling, as she so often did, at the beauty of Mother Earth, before going inside to check on Silk.

The barn was empty, completely deserted. Unease stirred in the back of her mind. She recalled her earlier feeling that she should wait for Silk to wake before going off. Mistflower wished now she had paid attention to it.

* * *

Silk was paralysed. He stared at the rapidly widening gap between his paws. The water seemed to fill up his whole head so that he couldn't think, couldn't see past the silent, yawning hole. Behind him he heard more pops and cracks and suddenly the ice he was standing on tilted, dropping him into the freezing water.

Overhead, Blackthorn voiced a startled cry.

Silk's head went under and for a long moment he sank like a

stone before his paws started automatically to move and he rose up through the dark, icy water until his head broke surface.

Silk trod water and mewed for his life.

Mistflower ran down the farmhouse path to the paddock where Larkspur, the plough horse, was contentedly munching hay and enjoying the sunshine. 'Have you seen Silk?'

Larkspur shook his head, snorting breath through his nostrils. 'He was asleep in the barn when Farmer John brought me down here.'

Sedgehop had not seen him either, nor had Berry, the Robin or Sharp Eye the Hare.

Unease was quickly turning to panic. What could she do? Where did she start looking? Storm! She needed Storm. If anybody would be able to help her, it would be him. Mistflower had an idea where he might be. At this time of day Storm was likely to be over in the south field, with Farmer John and the sheep. Mistflower hurried down the path, hoping desperately she was right; that Storm would be there.

Catching sight of Speckle, one of the Hens, she rushed over. 'Have you seen, Silk?'

'He's asleep, in the Barn.'

'No – I just looked and he's gone.'

Speckle continued her scratching in the dirt. 'Don't know then, I'm sure.'

Mistflower thanked her and carried on. Everywhere she looked, everyone she asked – there was no sign of him. The panic was out of control now, snapping at her heels like a hungry stoat.

What if Storm couldn't help her? What if Farmer John needed him to stay? Mistflower pushed the thought away and prayed to The Great God that all would be well and she was just worrying for nothing.

She was halfway to the south field when she saw Storm running hell for leather, toward her. Blackthorn was flying overhead.

'Quick!' Blackthorn called. 'The pond! Silk's fallen through the ice!'

'Climb aboard.' Storm paused only long enough for Mistflower to climb up onto his neck. 'Hold on tight.'

Mistflower grabbed a firm grip of his fur and they were off, running flat out toward the north field.

'I saw it happen,' Blackthorn told her. 'I went for Storm. I didn't know what else to do.'

As they raced toward the pond, Mistflower tried to still her fear and think. How had it happened? Why had Silk gone down there and then out onto the frozen water?

All was not lost – cats might not like water but they could swim, she reminded herself. Still she knew Silk didn't have long. Very quickly the cold would suck away his strength and he would simply … vanish.

'Find, Snowdrop.' Storm barked. 'Tell her to bring rope. There's some in the barn. Tell her to hurry.'

Blackthorn wheeled away from them and headed toward the farmhouse.

Mistflower tried to remember if she had seen Snowdrop the Swan that morning. Snowdrop liked to spend summer on the pond but she often went off for long stretches of time, especially during winter. Mistflower refused to consider what would happen if Snowdrop was not there.

She could see the pond up ahead now. Some of the animals had gathered around the edges. Lavender and Lilac were there and Mistflower could hear the unhappy and frightened lowing of Lilac, loud in the still air.

'Hurry up, Snowdrop.' Storm growled.

A sudden blur of wings and Blackthorn swooped down beside them.

'I found her, she's coming.'

'Has she got the rope, Blackthorn?'

Mistflower couldn't wait another moment. She ran down

Storm's front leg. 'I'm going out there.'

'*What* – no! It's dangerous out there. That crack could spread as quickly as someone turning on a tap. The whole thing could go – without any warning. And you're tiny. If you slip into that water, you'll be gone in an instant and we'll never find you.'

'I don't care, Storm! *Look*! Just look at him!'

Now they were closer they could clearly see Silk. He had long since stopped meowing, now he was barely moving. As they watched, his head slipped off the edge of the hole and he disappeared into the dark, cold water.

There was an agonizing wait, until finally, he fought his way back to the surface again. He was plainly exhausted.

Mistflower was afraid if he went under again, it would be the end of him.

'Hold on, Silk, begged Lilac. Hold on just a little bit longer. Blackthorn's gone for help.'

'*I'm coming Silk!*' Mistflower raced out onto the ice, her paws immediately going out from under her. 'I'm coming,' she called again as she slipped and slid her way across the surface of the pond.

'Where's Snowdrop? What's taking her so long?' Storm glanced around frantically.

Suddenly the swan glided past him without stopping, her powerful wings beating, carrying her toward the hole in the ice.

Storm let out a sharp yelp of relief. Trailing from Snowdrop's beak was the rope.

The word had spread and other animals had begun to gather. Storm could hear gasps and cries as they realised the seriousness of the situation. Despite the cold, Storm was panting.

Out on the ice, Mistflower had reached Silk. His chin barely rested on the edge of the hole and his green eyes were glazed. As she stared, his whole body shuddered and his chin began to slip.

'Silk!'

At the sound of her voice a flicker of life came back into Silk eyes but his chin continued to slip toward the hole.

'Silk, *please*! Stay with me. Please. Just a little longer – help's on its way.'

By a supreme effort, Silk pushed his chin further back on the ice. 'I'm cold,' he complained. 'I'm so cold.'

The rope just missed her as it fell to the ground.

'Grab it in your teeth, boy,' Snowdrop commanded. 'I'll have you out in a jiffy.'

Mistflower breathed a sigh of relief, thanking The Great God of All Things.

Snowdrop had aimed well, worn out as he was, Silk was still able to get the rope between his teeth.

'Hold tight,' Snowdrop called as she flew toward the waiting animals.

'Come on, Silk,' Mistflower urged. 'Big effort now and it'll all be over and we can get you warmed up again.'

'Get away from the water, Mistflower!' Storm barked. 'If the ice breaks any further, you're done for.'

Mistflower didn't know if it was what Storm had intended but his words roused Silk into action. As Snowdrop flew further away and the rope tightened, the brave little kitten scrabbled to get a grip on the frozen surface.

Again and again, his paws slipped of the edge, until finally, sides heaving, done for, he lay still.

His eyes fastened on hers and Mistflower could see death in them. Silk had given up.

'*No!*' She shouted. 'Don't give up, Silk. We'll get you out – just hold on. For me – just hold on!'

Storm was barking but she couldn't understand what he was saying. She knew if she took her attention off Silk, even for one instant, he would be gone.

She was aware of Snowdrop landing beside her, but still she couldn't risk looking away.

'I need you to move back now, Mistflower,' Snowdrop told

her.

'No! I'm staying right here.'

'If you want Silk to live, you'll do as I say.' Snowdrop kept her voice calm. 'I'm going to break the ice further, so I can get behind him and push him out. I can't do that while you're here.'

It was Silk's only chance, Mistflower knew it, but it took everything she had to obey.

'Hold on, Silk. Will you do that – for me – will you do that, Silk?' Her eyes were leaking and she didn't care. All she cared about at this moment was a black and white kitten who had come to be her heart in a way she could never have imagined.

There was no answer. Mistflower prayed Silk was just saving his strength.

She forced herself to move … one step … another … and then … she was running crazily … toward the waiting crowd.

The sound was like the crack the sticks made that men used to make the birds fall out of the sky. Mistflower glanced behind her as she reached the edge of the pond. The hole had more than doubled in size and still it grew larger and larger, the dark water eating up the surface of the pond.

Where was he! Mistflower's heart thud-thudded against her rib cage. She stared at the widening hole … *Nothing*! Silk was gone!

'No!' She screamed, watching as Snowdrop plunged into the freezing waters but it was too late. Silk had gone – sucked down into the icy depths.

Gathering Shadows

Horrified, she glanced at Storm but he didn't seem to understand. He had the rope between his teeth and his paws planted
firmly in the earth.

Mistflower swung her gaze back to the pond … and blinked.
Because … there he was! Mistflower forgot to breathe as once
again, Silk, with the rope still between his teeth, fought to get a
footing on the frozen surface. Snowdrop pushed and Storm
pulled with all his might and bit by bit, more and more of Silk
emerged from the hole.

The whole upper half of his body was free and Mistflower
had just begun to breathe again, when she heard another terrible
crack and the ice split apart, dunking Silk back into the water.

A collective gasp went up from the assembled animals.
Mistflower stared at the place where only moments ago Silk had
been. In that instant all hope died in her.

But it seemed, unlike her own abandonment, the Spirit of The
Great God living within Snowdrop had not given up on them
yet, because just then Snowdrop spread her mighty wings and

rose up out of the cold, black depths and hanging from her strong beak by the scruff of his neck was a soaking wet, beyond bedraggled, small, black and white kitten.

With a few powerful strokes, she deposited Silk beside Mistflower who stared at her, mute with gratitude.

Snowdrop gazed back, silent for a few moments, then, 'You,' she said, 'are a very strange mouse,' and stepping away from them both, she sailed off into the air.

'Come on, youngling,' Storm said, his eyes on the shivering, exhausted kitten. 'We'd better get you home – we need to get you warmed up before you catch the sneezes.'

Mistflower turned to Storm. 'How are we going to get him home?' It was plain Silk had used up all of his strength getting out of the hole.

Storm gave her a long look. 'He's going to run home, Mistflower. And I'm going to make sure he gives it all he's got.'

'He's already given all he's got,' Mistflower snapped. She couldn't believe Storm could be so cruel.

Storm sighed. 'We need to warm him up, *now*! Because if we don't, the time he's spent in that water, I don't hold out much hope of him not coming down with something bad – something really bad. And if I'm ill, or any of the farm animals, Farmer John gets someone to help us.' He dropped his voice to a little above a whisper. 'I don't think we can count on him doing the same for a stray kitten, do you?

'So if you've got any better ideas, you just let me know.'

Mistflower stared at Silk; pity for his condition and the necessity of getting him warm fought each other in her head. After a brief space she hardened her heart.

'You heard Storm – get running.'

She thought he would argue, and the fact he didn't almost caused her to break, but Silk, obedient as ever, dragged himself to his paws and took an unsteady step, followed by another and another.

'Pick it up!' Storm's voice was merciless but a glance at his face told Mistflower it was hurting him to do this just as much as it was hurting her.

When Silk failed to increase his pace, Storm growled low in his throat, baring his teeth and snapping at the small cat's sodden fur.

Startled, confused, at the end of his tether, the miserable kitten stumbled into a weaving, wavering run. His sides heaved and the tip of his pink tongue poked from his mouth.

The north field was not a huge field and in the end, getting home couldn't really have taken that long, but for Mistflower it was the longest journey of her life.

Somehow Silk managed to stay on his feet until they had almost reached home. By that time though, he had slowed to walking pace and Storm and Mistflower had given up trying to keep him to a run. Just in sight of the barn his strength finally gave out and Storm picked him up by the scruff of the neck and carried him inside.

Lilac, had stayed close by Silk throughout the awful journey, now she went and lay down in a corner of the barn, away from draughts and a little warmer. 'Come and lie down here, Silk,' she said. 'I'll help you get dry.'

Silk staggered to his paws again and dragged himself over to her. He curled up, pressed tight against her warmth and lay there, shivering.

Storm had disappeared as soon as they got back, suddenly he reappeared, carrying a small, neatly folded blanket in his mouth. He dropped it over Silk and carefully arranged it to cover the freezing kitten.

'Is that Peanut's old blanket?' Lavender asked. 'How did you get hold of that?'

'Miss Lucy put it in the outhouse when Peanut stopped needing it. I thought youngling could do with it.'

Lavender planted a kiss on the top of Storm's head. 'You're

the best, you are.'

Storm's tail wagged. 'Well, we've all got a wonderful example to learn from,' he said, looking at Mistflower, anxiously watching over Silk. 'Don't you think?'

Lavender sighed. 'He'll be all right, won't he, Storm?'

'He's young and he's strong – as for the rest, that's for The Great God to decide. We can only do what we can.' Storm fell silent. After a moment he said, 'What I'd like to know is what he was doing out there? He's never gone any further than the farmyard since the day they moved in here. Why would he take it into his head to go to the north field today?'

'Well – maybe he just decided to explore. He's only a kitten after all, and kittens do get into mischief.

'You remember when Miss Lucy first brought Peanut home? He was into everything! D'you remember when he got himself stuck in the oak tree at the bottom of the lane? And Farmer John had to get the ladder and climb up and bring him down.' Lavender laughed. 'And that time he got that plastic bag wound round his neck – that could've been nasty, you know, if you hadn't spotted him and run for Miss Lucy.' Lavender sighed again. 'I miss him.'

Storm grinned. 'Me too. And I know Miss Lucy does – I think that's why she's never got another kitten. She's still too full of remembering him.

'Anyway, I'd best get back or Farmer John will wonder where I am – and we don't want him coming to look for me in the barn, do we?

'You keep an eye on things here, Lavender. Send someone to get me if you need help.'

As word got around more and more animals drifted into the barn to check on Silk and offer Mistflower words of reassurance.

'He's a fighter,' Strawberry, one of the chickens told her. 'He's going to be just fine, you'll see – stop your worrying or it's you who'll end up sick.'

Mistflower was overcome by everyone's kindness but she didn't miss the fact that one animal had not called by to see how Silk was. One animal, even as dusk gathered and the Sun dropped below the horizon, was still missing from the welcoming barn.

* * *

Lilac's body was as warm as an oven. You could almost see the steam rising of Silk. Very quickly he was asleep. Not long after, his paws began jerking and soft, frightened mews escaped from his throat as his whiskers twitched.

Silk was dreaming. In his dream he was back, standing on the edge of the pond. Behind him a large shadow sped ever closer. Try as he might, Silk couldn't see anything else except the shadow looming over him.

Although he didn't know what it was, he was scared, more afraid than he'd ever been in his life. In a moment, he knew it would catch up with him and then ... something bad was going to happen. Every fibre of him wanted to run but, for some reason, the only way he could go was across the pond ... and the pond frightened him even more than the dark shadow did.

Silk awoke with a terrified mew.

'It's all right, Silk.' Lilac's familiar voice cut through his fear. 'I'm here. You can sleep safe.'

Silk nestled himself even closer and between one breath and another, was asleep again.

The next time he opened his eyes he was dry and warm once more and very, very hungry. Lilac, true to her words, was exactly where she had been when he'd curled up and gone to sleep. Silk started purring.

'Are ... are you awake, Silk?' Lilac whispered, just in case he wasn't.'

'I'm awake.'

'How are you feeling?'

Silk turned his head toward the sound of Mistflower's voice.

'Much better now, thank you, especially with you and Lilac here.'

'Where else would we be?' Mistflower's voice was soft. 'You're our very best friend.'

Silk purred again. The shock of what had happened was slowly fading and being surrounded by his friends made him feel safe and happy. Giving a great big yawn, he got to his paws and str-et-ched luxuriously.

Sometime during the evening Storm had carried his bowl down to the barn. In it was a good measure of left over stew the Farmer's wife had made for lunch and Silk wasted no time in helping himself to some of it.

Mistflower and Lilac watched him eat. He was just finishing up when Lavender came over.

'Well,' she said. 'You're looking more like yourself again.'

'I'm feeling much better,' Silk said and burped delicately. 'Oops – s-orry!'

'What happened, Silk?' Mistflower asked. 'Why did you go out onto the pond?'

'Caramel told me to,' Silk said, sneezing.

'That – that – cow!' Lavender mooed, angry. 'I should've guessed she'd have something to do with it! Just wait till I get hold of her!'

'But why did you do as she said, Silk?' Storm had slipped into the barn unnoticed.

Mistflower thought that was a very good question.

'I had to,' Silk said. 'Caramel told me Mistflower was in trouble and I had to be quick. She said going across the pond was the quickest way to get to the woods.' Silk sneezed again.

Storm gave a low growl. 'Wait till I see that Missie.'

Mistflower ran up Silk's leg, onto his head, placing a kiss on his nose. 'I love you, Silk,' she said. All they had been through.

All they had shared, she had never told him that before. She realised the telling was long past due.

'I – I love you too, Mistflower,' Silk said shyly. He glanced at Lilac and Lavender, finally at Storm. 'I – I love you all.' He sneezed again.

Mistflower threw him a worried look. Since Silk's first sneeze she had been trying to tell herself it was nothing, just cold water getting up his nose – that was all. But there was a part of her that already knew different.

She could sense the sickness in him, like a grey shadow covering his light. She knew what that grey shadow meant. She had seen it before in sick animals. She saw from the way they were looking at him Lavender and Storm could sense it too.

Even Lilac, although she didn't recognise what it was, could feel something was not right. She skittered nervously around Silk, switching her tail, though the barn was empty of flies.

Mistflower fought to hold down her rising alarm. He's young, she told herself, echoing Strawberries words. He's strong.

Storm's eyes locked on hers. Steady, they seemed to say. One step at a time gets the journey done.

Mistflower took a deep, steadying breath. She had seen the shadow in animals who became well again, she reminded herself. Silk's race was not yet run.

Silk was thirsty. He wandered over to Larkspur's trough and drank a little water before going back to his blanket. He ached all over. He supposed it was the bitter chill of the dark water still inside his bones, that and straining to get out.

He must remember to thank Snowdrop next time he saw her. He shuddered, thinking about what would have happened if it hadn't been for her.

He hardly recalled the trek home, except for how tired he had been and how cold and the way Storm and Mistflower had pushed him on when all he wanted to do was lie down and let the cold win. He knew they had made him keep fighting because they loved him and didn't want the cold to succeed.

Silk yawned and sneezed. He was growing sleepy again. Soon he slept.

* * *

Dusk had put away her cloak and Night had shaken out her shawl by the time Caramel dared to show her face in the barn.

'I can't *believe* you've got the nerve to come in here!' Lavender lowed.

'I – I almost didn't.' Caramel confessed. 'But it's so cold and … dark … out there … all alone.'

'Well – if you think—'

'Why'd you do it, Caramel?' Storm interrupted.

'D – do what?'

Storm growled. 'Don't play games with me, Missie, or you'll live to regret it.'

'I only wanted to help.' Caramel said in a small voice.

'Help! That's a laugh.' Lavender was angrier than she had ever been in her life. 'You wouldn't help Silk and Mistflower if your own tail depended on it!'

'Well?' Storm growled again.

'I – I knew you'd all think the worst. That's why I was frightened to come home.' Caramel lowered her head.

'I know I was against them at the start, but,' she glanced at Storm, 'after you talked to me about them coming here to live, well, things changed. I saw how much a part of our family they'd become and I – my feelings changed. Not that I expect you to believe me,' she finished.

'How is it? Storm said. 'That you came to *help* young Silk onto the frozen pond?' Storm shook his head. 'For goodness sake, you had to know it was unsafe!'

'I – I didn't!' Caramel insisted. 'He's such a little thing, I thought he'd be all right. I thought the ice would hold. Oh – you've got to believe me!' Caramel pleaded.

Storm could see Caramel's distress was real. He only wished he could be as certain about her story.

'You've still to explain to me why you would've sent him there,' he said.

'I – I was in the woods, I just wanted a bit of time to myself, you know?' Caramel looked at Storm but if she was hoping for some kind of response, an indication he was softening toward her, she was disappointed.

'Anyway,' she hurried on. 'Out of the corner of my eye, I saw a flash of something and I saw a hawk, giving chase. I thought it must be Mistflower he was after. I – I just panicked. I didn't know what to do – so I ran back to the barn – I was looking for you, Storm. But I couldn't find you.

'There was no one around, except Silk – and he was asleep. So I woke him up and told him Mistflower needed his help and that the quickest way was across the pond.'

'I don't believe you.' Lavender glared at her. 'You're lying! You know Mistflower is under Ghost's protection.'

'I do – but the hawk might not have. I couldn't be sure.'

Caramel turned to Storm. 'Am I to be cast out because Lavender refuses to see the truth when it's staring at her?' she asked.

For a long moment Storm was silent. He didn't believe Caramel either. Every instinct he had told him she was false. But to take such a serious step as banishing her from the barn he had to be absolutely certain. He needed proof beyond a doubt.

He looked at Lavender, standing ready to butt horns. 'We have to give her the benefit of the doubt.'

'What? You can't possibly believe her, Storm! You know what she said when we voted to let Silk and Mistflower come here to live. She said she'd kill them first and—'

'We have to give her the benefit of the doubt, Lavender.' Storm repeated gently but firmly.

He could understand how she felt. He was half inclined to throw his sense of duty to the wind and follow his gut as well. He sighed. Caramel had been trouble from being a calf. He couldn't figure it out really, she had come from Honey, one of the nicest tempered cows anyone could ever wish to meet. Honey would have shared her last blade of grass if needed.

Reluctantly, Lavender moved aside and let Caramel pass.

Storm watched her go. From now on he would be minding her as carefully as a worm minds a bird. If she put one hoof wrong, he would be on her.

He knew Mistflower was watching him and had heard everything. Storm felt as if he had let the courageous little mouse down. It was an uncomfortable feeling but he had a job to do, a responsibility.

Farmer John relied on him to take care of the animals and he couldn't allow himself to fail in his role, no matter how he might personally feel. Unlikely though it seemed, there was just a small chance Caramel was telling them the truth.

Dark Skies

By morning Silk's nose was hot and runny and he was sneezing all the time. His eyes were watery, his appetite had disappeared and he hurt all over. His legs were so weak he could barely stand and all he wanted to do was sleep.

Mistflower and Lilac stayed by his side all day. Mistflower could see the shadow in him had grown larger over night and that his light had burnt down to nothing more than a tiny spark.

Around mid-day Lavender persuaded Lilac and her to have a break. 'He'll be fine,' she said. 'I won't leave his side for a second until you get back. Now go away – get something to eat and a bit of fresh air.'

Mistflower didn't want food, instead she wandered outside. She had slept badly and today, as never before, she felt old and tired and fretful. Fear was all over her. She could taste it and smell it and feel it. She knew if she couldn't conquer it she would be of little use to Silk, now, or if he lived, in the future.

Finding a comfortable patch of grass not too far from the door she settled herself down. The Sun was warm on her fur. Closing her eyes she lifted her face, bathing in the golden rays.

Please Great God, the words sprang to her mind from somewhere deep within. *Let him live! If you must have a life, take mine. My journey has been long and rich and ... I don't want to have to live without Silk. Take me,* she pleaded.

She didn't know if she had been heard but she knew Silk's life was now, as always, in the hands of a higher power.

Caramel had left in the early morning, after a tense night spent being given the silent treatment by the other animals. But Mistflower was alert, ready to rush back to Silk at the first glimpse of her.

Mistflower felt sorry for Storm, it was a difficult situation for him, but if she were honest, she wished he had chased Caramel off. She didn't for one instant believe the big, tan coloured, cow's story and she feared they would never be safe as long as Caramel was around.

* * *

Silk hovered in that twilight place, between waking and sleeping, all day. Storm carried his bowl to the barn. In it was savoury mince, Silk's favourite, but Silk didn't raise himself from his blanket to take even the smallest piece.

The animals all did their best, stopping by where Silk lay to keep company with the little group, trying hard to raise Mistflower's spirits but it was clear from their manner they all saw the same shadow she could see.

Snowdrop had called by several times. 'He'll be all right,' she told Mistflower, the first time she came. 'He's a fighter, that one. He would never have made it out of that hole if he hadn't been.'

The day passed slowly and as darkness painted the sky, Mistflower fell into an exhausted sleep.

The next time she opened her eyes it was early morning. She

immediately checked on Silk.

'It's all right, Lilac whispered. I've been watching him – I couldn't sleep. He's all right.'

'Thank you, Lilac.' Mistflower said, relieved. She had only meant to have a little snooze and although she didn't think Caramel would try anything with all the other animals in the barn, especially Storm, she couldn't help feeling guilty for staying asleep all night.

'I've been watching him too,' Storm spoke quietly, not wanting to disturb the sleeping Silk. 'He's holding his own.'

Mistflower looked carefully. Storm was right, the shadow had not grown any overnight and Silk's light, though faint, still shone steadily.

The Sun had climbed high over the horizon before Silk made his unsteady way to Larkspur's trough and cautiously lowering his head, drank deeply. Finished, he sat down where he was, gazing around himself thoughtfully.

'How are you feeling?' Mistflower asked.

'Better,' Silk told her. 'My legs are all bendy in the wrong places and my head feels full of cotton wool, but better.'

Mistflower gave him a long, searching look and indeed, she could see the shadow was smaller now and Silk's light was bigger and brighter than it had been.

'Thanks be to The Great God of All Things,' she said, breathing a sigh of relief.

'I was wondering.' Silk tilted his head a little to one side. 'I always have to hide when Farmer John comes into the barn. Hasn't he been in lately?'

Usually, if they had some warning Farmer John was on his way, Silk would run outside and hide. If the farmer came upon them suddenly, one of the animals would distract his attention while Silk slipped behind the bales of hay or the tractor wheel. There was no shortage of places in the barn to hide from a human.

'Don't you worry your sweet self about that.' Mistflower ran up his leg and placed a kiss on the top of his head. 'We just covered you over with the blanket and he didn't notice a thing.'

'Oh. It's a good job I didn't sneeze while he was here.'

Mistflower caught her breath. It was, without a doubt, lucky. No one had thought about that … again, The Great God had favoured them.

Silk, making a determined effort, rose to his paws and crossed the floor to where Storm's bowl stood. The sheepdog had left it half full of the stew the farmer's wife had put down for his breakfast that morning.

Silk sniffed at it delicately before picking at a few small pieces. He lapped up some of the hearty gravy before returning to his blanket and settling down.

Just then, Lilac, who had been marched out of the door by her concerned mother and told, in no uncertain terms, she was not to return to the barn until she had spent some time in the fresh air, galloped back into the barn, tail held high.

'Silk!' You're awake! Are you better?

'He's a little better,' Mistflower said. 'But he's still very weak and tired, Lilac. He'll need to get his rest for the next few days.'

'Oh.' Lilac looked crest fallen. I won't tire him out,' she said. 'I promise. I'll just stay right here with him until he's ready to play out again.' And she settled herself down beside Silk, exactly where she had been since he had first fallen ill.

'I'll stay with him, Lilac,' Mistflower told her. 'You go and kick up your heels a bit. You're only a youngling yourself. You must get bored lying there all day with nothing to do.'

Lilac turned liquid brown eyes toward her. 'If you don't mind, I'd rather stay here.'

Mistflower smiled to herself. Silk was very easy to love.

In a few moments the subject of their conversation was asleep again, one paw resting on Lilac's nose.

Mistflower felt the weight of the last few days slip from her shoulders. The Great God in his mercy had seen fit to grant Silk his life. Mistflower didn't think she could have gone on if she had lost him. Losing Sage had almost been her undoing and to lose someone she loved with all her heart again would surely have been the end of her.

It took Silk another two days to fully recover his strength and by the end of three weeks he seemed to have put what had happened out of his mind completely. So much so that Mistflower decided to have a talk with him. She waited until they were alone together and started off by asking about his health.

'You know I'm feeling better.' Silk placed a gentle kiss on the top of her head. 'That's not really what you want to talk to me about, is it?'

Mistflower gave the black and white cat a slow, measuring look. Somewhere along the line, she realised, Silk had grown from a scruffy little bag of bones to a sleek and handsome, young cat. Just when it had happened she couldn't quite recall but she did recall his courage in going after her, without hesitation, when he thought she was in trouble and needing his help.

She remembered his bravery in the dark, icy waters of the pond. She thought about the uncomplaining way he had struggled home, shocked and exhausted though he was. There had not been one word of reproach from him since that day, to Storm or herself, for the way they had pushed him until he collapsed.

Silk was still looking at her, waiting for her to speak.

'I just wanted to tell you to be very careful around Caramel. Lavender and Storm had it out with her ... for sending you across the pond ... she had a good enough story but ... I'm—'

'You're not sure if you believe her,' Silk interrupted.

'N-o,' Mistflower said, slowly. 'I'm not sure I do.'

'Why would she try to harm me, Mistflower?' There was hurt and confusion in Silk's green eyes. 'I've never done anything to her.

'I don't know, Silk. I don't have any answers for you. Except to warn you against being alone with her. You never know, perhaps what she told Lavender and Storm was true and it was all just a terrible accident ... and I'm just being suspicious over nothing.'

In her heart Mistflower didn't for one moment believe Caramel's story. But she could see how much it pained Silk to think Caramel would do such a dreadful thing.

'Come on,' she said, running up his leg to sit behind his ear. 'Let's go for a walk.'

* * *

Caramel trudged around the middle field. She was feeling very sorry for herself. No one was speaking to her and for Caramel there was no worse punishment imaginable. She had never felt so alone in her life. Worse still, that mangy moggie and the mad mouse were both still alive and still living in the barn. Caramel despaired of ever getting rid of them. Storm and Lavender were watching her as closely as a mother watches her calf.

It just wasn't fair! She had been happy before those two ragged rascals had come into her life. Right from the first day she had met them, they had been nothing but a thorn in her side.

Well – she wasn't ready to give up just yet. Everyone might be on her back like a pack of wolves but she had a plan. She would get rid of Silk and Mistflower yet. All she needed was a little bit of help and she knew just where to go for that – well – perhaps not the exact spot.

Lifting her head, she spotted Berry, the Robin. 'Ah! He would know.'

'Berry,' she mooed quickly. 'Can you tell me where Longtooth's burrow is, please?'

But Berry ignored her and carried on flying.

Rage and self-pity fought each other as Caramel watched him

fly away. 'Just you wait!' She muttered. 'Revenge is a dish best served cold.' She wasn't absolutely certain what that meant but she had heard Farmer John's wife say it once in a grim tone of voice and somehow, it seemed to fit her situation.

'You looking for me?'

Startled, Caramel almost leaped out of her skin. She had been so lost in her thoughts she had failed to notice Longtooth.

The badger eyed Caramel suspiciously. 'What d'you want with me?'

'Oh – I, I just wanted a little chat.'

'My – how the mighty have fallen.' Longtooth laughed. 'Are you so desperate to talk to someone you've come to search me out?'

Caramel itched to lash out with one of her hooves and land a good, hard kick on the badger's snout. Instead she forced herself to coolness. 'I don't know what you're talking about.'

Longtooth laughed again. 'Well – what is it you want? Quick now – I've better things to do than stand round here, chatting with you.'

'Do you have to be so rude?' Caramel was fast losing patience.

'Beggars can't be choosers – and rumour has it you've run out of friends.'

Any moment now, Caramel thought, and I'm going to trample you under my hooves and dance a jig on your broken bones.

'I've a little proposition for you,' she said.

'Proposition? What's that when it's at home?'

'You stu – are you going to hear me out or not?'

'Go on then, I'm listening aren't I?'

Caramel pushed down her loathing of the badger. 'I want you to do something for me,' she said.

This time Longtooth laughed long and hard. 'And why would I be doing anything for the likes of you?'

'Because if you don't, I'm going to tell Storm that you and your cubs are living in this field ... and you know how farmers feel about badgers coming near their cattle.

'Farmer John will tear your sett apart and he won't stop until you're all dead.'

'You – you wouldn't!' But even as she said it, Longtooth knew the truth. A chill ran down her spine. This was a creature who had not hesitated in leading a youngling out to what should have been certain death. She would not show mercy to a badger and her cubs.

'W-what do you want from me?'

'Nothing much, dear. Just a little thing, really.' Caramel's ears twitched. She glanced around herself, lowering her voice.

'I want you to get rid of that moth eaten moggie.'

'*What*? And how exactly am I supposed to do that?'

'I don't know – that's for you to work out. But I want him dead. Understand? I want him gone – deceased – dead.

'I don't care how you do it – just *do* it! Make no mistake, Longtooth, it's either him or you and your cubs.'

'Why do you hate him so much?'

Caramel's ears twitched again. She pawed the earth.

'I hate him because from the first instant I saw him, he took away my authority. The herd had always looked to me as their leader. Oh – it was unspoken but it was there nevertheless and then that mange bag and the rotten rodent arrived and suddenly everything changed. Cows started to question my position. They started arguing with things I said and ignoring my rules and doing what they pleased.'

Caramel stared at Longtooth, eyes wild. 'They – they ruined my life,' she said, breathing hard.

Longtooth looked at the creature before her. She had no wish to harm the kitten but she could see no way out.

'Won't they be watching you?' she said, playing for time.

'That's exactly it!' Caramel crowed. 'They'll be watching ME – not you. So you'll be free to do whatever you want with it.'

'It?'

'The *kitten*, you idiot! Do whatever you want with the kitten!'

Longtooth glanced away from Caramel, her thoughts in a whirl. She would pretend to go along with the plan, she decided. But she wouldn't actually do anything – just stall until her cubs were bigger and they could all move away and make a new home somewhere else.

As if she had read her mind, Caramel said, 'You've got two days. After that, I'm going to Storm and you and your cubs are finished.' She danced nervously on the spot for an instant before galloping away across the field, tail high, as if all the creatures of the shadow world were after her.

For a stretch of time, Longtooth stared after her. Fear was a stench in her nostrils. It was a gripping pain in her guts and a chill wind on the back of her neck. It was a foul taste in her mouth. Suddenly she turned and dashed back to her home and her cubs.

All day she couldn't settle. Her cubs quickly picked up her fear and crawled over her restlessly, refusing to leave her side, even when it was time for her to hunt. But that didn't bother Longtooth, she wasn't hungry anyway. Every time she tried to think, the only thing that came into her head was a red tide of fear.

By next morning Longtooth had accepted her fate. Another few weeks and her cubs would be old enough for her to move them. But to attempt it now would be as good as killing them. There was no way out for her. The cow had spoken true; it was either the youngling or her own babies.

She was going to have to do this terrible thing, this crime against Mother Nature and The Great God of All Things. Longtooth shuddered and The Great God help her if Ghost ever found out what she had done.

The face of Evil

All day she forced herself to carry on as usual. She nursed her cubs and spent the time playing with them and making sure they were content.

When night fell she made herself go out to hunt and eat, she had to stay strong – for her cubs. Their lives depended on her. If she didn't feed, her milk would dry up and they would die anyway and his dreadful thing she must do would be for nothing.

When the Sun rose on the third day, Longtooth had her plan. Many times in the early morn, just as she was returning home, she had witnessed the youngling wander down to the fence at the top of her field.

This morning she would lie in wait, in the bushes at the corner of the fence and when he appeared she would chase him. She would run him right across the field. She would chase him hard, so he had no space to collect himself, until they reached the drop on the other side of the woods.

76

She would chase him until he fell, right over the edge, to his death – and may the Great God forgive her.

Hidden beneath the bushes, Longtooth fretted and waited. Perhaps she had delayed too long? What if the youngling didn't come this morning? What if she failed? There would be no mercy from Caramel, of that she could be sure. Lost in her tormented thoughts, Longtooth finally spotted Silk, strolling unhurriedly down the path toward her.

Seeing him, equal parts of misery and relief warred in her. She desperately wished there was something else she could do, another choice she could make. Longtooth knew what she did here today would stay with her until her own death and that from this day forward she would never be the same again.

Steeling herself, Longtooth burst from cover snarling, launching herself at the startled Silk. She bore down on him, a furry killing machine, tooth and nail ready to draw blood.

Silk did the only thing he could – he ran – through the fence and into the field. At first he was more shocked than truly afraid. As he ran he reasoned the badger must have attacked because she was afraid of him and if he put some space between them she would see he wasn't going to hurt her and let him be.

Halfway across the field he realised his mistake and fear began to drive him faster. He was running blindly now, not thinking, just tearing across the grass, needing to get away from the badger on his back.

Silk could hear the animal crashing through the dense vegetation. He streaked through the woods, only recognizing he could have climbed to safety as he passed the last few saplings, leaving the trees behind him as he sprinted for open ground.

He risked a quick glance behind and saw the badger had closed the gap between them. He was running flat out now, nothing left to give.

His whole world had narrowed to the strip of earth marking his path as he tried desperately to increase the distance between them. The grass was long and soaked with dew but he barely registered the fact as he pounded along.

The next instant he heard himself scream as something snapped at his back leg, fastening its terrible jaws around his flesh.

Silk was caught. Dazed, he tried again to run but his leg was held fast and a dreadful pain was eating its way through the bone.

He couldn't understand it – how had the badger run him down when he hadn't even seen her close on him? He was suddenly weak all over and trembling, as if a mighty hand had grabbed onto him by the scruff of the neck and was shaking ... shaking.

Something was wrong with his eyes ... everything was growing dark. Suddenly all sense left him and he fell to the ground, unmoving.

Longtooth gazed at what she had done in utter disgust. Never before had she felt ashamed of herself like this. She had lived her whole life according to the Law.

Even now her mind searched for some other way to go but it was hopeless and ... already too late. The youngling's leg was bleeding badly and shock had taken a grip of him. Very soon, she knew, his life would flow from him the way the blood flowed from his wound.

Sick at heart, Longtooth turned away. There was nothing she could do and she had to get back to her cubs. She had already been away too long and they would be cold and afraid.

She glanced behind herself one last time. The thought came to her that the young cat would die also, cold, alone and afraid.

Longtooth ran. It'll be over soon, she thought, as she ran. It'll be over and the poor thing will never have to be afraid again.

* * *

'Something's happened to him,' Mistflower said, her voice choked with dread. 'Something's happened to him! I know it.'

They had been out searching for hours. Blackthorn, Berry, Hurricane and Gale had scoured the land to all sides. They had gone down to the pond. They had searched the fields right up to the road – there was absolutely no sign of Silk. It was as if he had vanished into thin air.

'Steady now, Mistflower.' Storm soothed. 'We don't *know* anything yet.' But the worry showed plain in his voice.

'H-he wouldn't have taken off for this long, Storm.' Mistflower tried hard to keep herself from flying apart. 'You know he wouldn't.

'Oh … *where* can he be?'

Storm couldn't quite meet her eyes. Nor could Lavender and Lilac was in a worse state than she herself was.

The thing they had all so far avoided saying. The thing they all believed to be true was that Caramel had again done something to Silk. Yet, how could she have? She had barely left the barn for days now. Still Mistflower could not rid herself of the feeling that something bad had happened to her very best friend in all the world and that Caramel had everything to do with it.

Mistflower fought the urge to find Caramel, run up her leg, sink her teeth into her nose and hang on with all her might until she succeeded in making her confess. That was a sure road to having her brains beaten out against the wall, as well as losing any chance to catch Caramel off guard.

'We'll search again at first light tomorrow.' Storm knew if they hadn't found him today there wasn't much chance they would find him tomorrow but there was nothing else he could think of to offer Mistflower in the way of comfort.

He saw from the defeated manner in which she turned away from him, Mistflower had already arrived at the same conclusion, but it was the only thin hope they had left.

* * *

Silk opened his eyes on darkness. For an instant he thought they were playing tricks on him again, then he realised the Moon was sailing the clouds.

His back leg had settled down to a deep, aching throb and he was cold – almost as cold as he had been in the deep and icy waters of the pond. The world around him drifted in and out of focus and his awareness drifted with it so that one moment he was lying on the ground, feeling the steady pain eating into his thigh and the next he had fallen into a black bottomless pit and then back, lying on the ground again.

Around him was total silence, not a thing moved. Silk forced his heavy head up, glancing about himself. He was lying in long grass at the base of a solitary elder tree and he realised now, whatever it was biting into his leg, was not a living creature at all, it was some manmade thing, fashioned out of the same material as Farmer John's tractor.

He knew he should call out, perhaps some animal would hear him and tell his friends but try as he might, he just could not find the strength.

Why was it, he asked himself? He had never done anything to hurt anyone, yet someone had tied him in a plastic bag and thrown him away like so much rubbish.

He could clearly remember how horrible it had been, how frightening and confusing, how the air had grown bad and it had become hard to breathe and how desperate he had been when he had started to claw his way out of there. Even this, being caught like this and in awful pain, was better than being inside that bag … and Caramel hated him … and now that badger had attacked him for no reason, had run him into the contraption that had sunk its teeth into his leg.

Why? Why did they all hate him? What was it he had done to make them want to hurt him … he just didn't understand it at all.

He carried that thought down with him, into the darkness of the pit.

The next time Silk awoke, the Elder Sylph was covering him with old leaves.

'They'll keep the rain off you,' she told him.

Silk marvelled at the sound of her voice, it was as if he heard a soft summer breeze rustling through the boughs of the trees in her words. He wanted to thank her but before he could the pit yawned opened again and swallowed him up.

* * *

Longtooth had spent the worst night of her life. At first light, when she should have been settling down to sleep, despite telling herself it was exactly the wrong thing to do, she slipped back through the wood; to the place where the young cat lay.

What drove her was the need to know his suffering had ended. She wanted to be sure it was all done with and he was at peace now and that only she was left in torment.

She sniffed cautiously as she slowly approached the youngling. He was still alive! She could see his light, very faint, a tiny spark, but still there. She felt his agony like a knife in her own heart.

'This is wrong, Longtooth.'

Longtooth jumped at the Sylph's voice.

'It's a terrible thing you do.'

Longtooth could not look at her. 'I – I know.' Her voice trembled. 'I've no choice.'

'There is always choice, Longtooth.'

'D'you expect me to kill my own babies? Because, if I don't do this, then that's what'll happen … they'll die and their deaths will be on my head. Isn't it better to let one creature die then let my own babies go to their deaths?'

The Elder Sylph sighed, a sound like dried leaves dancing in the wind. 'The death of your cubs is not certain. It is in the hands of The Great God. The death of Silk, is certain – and it falls on your head, Longtooth.'

The Sylph ran her hand gently along the unconscious Silk's body. She looked at Longtooth. Her long russet coloured hair was dressed with leaves and berries and a garland of white elder-flowers decorated her throat. Her dress shimmered with hues of green, which changed and shifted into purples and golds. Her bark brown eyes glistened with unshed tears. 'He thinks you hate him,' she said, sadly. 'And he doesn't know why ... what he's done to offend you.'

Longtooth could stand it no more. She turned away, retracing her steps.

'Remember,' the Sylph called. 'There's always choice.'

Longtooth knew she spoke true. She flattened her ears. She didn't know why this had come to her – but she knew what she had to do.

Her cubs were crying for her when she reached home. Longtooth gave them milk and played with them until they eventually fell asleep.

She watched them sleeping, long and long. They were not her first litter but her love for them was no less fierce for that. Longtooth had never before hated another living creature. It was a completely new and wholly consuming feeling.

The Sun was riding high by the time she left her sett and began to make her way to the barn.

* * *

'He's gone, isn't he?' Mistflower forced the words from her grief locked throat. 'He's gone and ... he's never coming back again.'

Storm whined unhappily. 'We can't give up on him, Mistflower.'

Mistflower said nothing but Storm could feel her despair. He searched his mind for some words of comfort and came up blank. Truth to tell, he couldn't find much hope inside himself.

'Come on,' he barked. 'Let's check the barn. If he's still not back we'll try the woods again. Silently, the two made for home. Storm knew he wasn't offering much, Sedgehop or one of the hens would have come running if Silk had turned up.

Everyone had been searching since first light. Blackthorn, Berry, Hurricane and Gale between them had covered further than the rest of them could ever have managed on foot. Snowdrop had scoured along the pond ways and right out to the river that ran, many miles south of Farmer John's land.

Even Caramel had joined in the hunt for Silk. Storm had his own opinion on that but he kept it to himself. Now was not the time for anger. Now they needed to work as a team. Yet, despite all their efforts, it was as if Mother Earth herself had swallowed the youngling up.

'What?' Storm shot a look at Mistflower.

'I – I don't know.'

Stood outside the barn door, in broad daylight, was Longtooth, the badger.

Storm padded toward her. All he could think was she must have news of Silk.

'Storm,' she said, surprising him by using his name. 'I need to tell you something.'

Lightning Strikes

'I know it must mean nothing to you,' Longtooth finished. 'But I'm truly sorry.'

'The biggest shame is, it was all for nothing.' Storm shook himself. 'I knew you and your cubs were there. Oh – don't mistake me. If I thought for one moment you or they were a danger to Farmer John's herd, I would've moved you on long ago. But you kept yourself to yourself and the cattle don't pasture in the middle field – I couldn't see any harm in letting well alone.'

Storm glanced at Mistflower. 'Seems I was wrong after all.'

'It's not you should be sorry,' Mistflower said, speaking to Longtooth. 'You did what any mother would do – you protected your babes.' She held the badger's startled gaze. 'Thank you for telling us. You've been very brave. Go back to your cubs now.'

Longtooth looked at Storm. 'I would ask a boon? I would ask for one more month. If I move us out now, my cubs will die. They're too young.'

Storm growled.

'You and your family are safe as far as we're concerned.'

Mistflower told her. 'The responsibility for this lies on someone else's head.'

'Y ...' Storm was afraid to hear the answer but he had to ask. 'You're sure he's still alive.'

Longtooth hung her head in shame. 'He was still clinging to life when I saw him this morning,' she said, her voice full of regret.

Mistflower was already perched and holding firm to the fur behind Storm's ear. 'Run,' she squeaked. 'As fast as you like.'

Storm ran like the wind and in no time at all they were through the woods and heading for the lone elder tree.

Even up close it was difficult to see him – he was lying directly beneath the tree, hidden by the long grass and buried under a carpet of leaves.

'Small wonder no one spotted him,' panted Storm.

Mistflower threw herself from his neck, hitting the ground at a run. She sprinted swiftly up onto the top of Silk's head and peered down into his open eyes. 'Silk!'

'M-Mistflower? Is it really you? Am I just dreaming?'

'Oh ... Silk ... my sweet, sweet boy! Look what she's done to you!'

'Why does everyone hate me, Mistflower?'

'Sssh, Silk, what a thing to say when you have so many who love you so dearly.'

'That badger attacked me for nothing!'

'Yes – I know, Silk. But she was afraid for her cubs.'

'Cubs? I didn't go near her cubs! I didn't even know she had any!'

'It was Caramel put her up to it,' Storm growled. 'She told Longtooth she'd tell me they were living in the middle field. She told her Farmer John would kill them all.'

'*She* hates me!'

Mistflower huffed. 'That cow hates everything. I don't even think she likes herself. How can she, when she acts the way she does?'

Silk was quiet for a moment, then, 'It's not just her though. Someone put me in a plastic bag and threw me away. They wanted me to die. Why? Why would someone do that? I'm not a bad cat – I've never hurt a thing.'

Mistflower kissed the tip of his nose. 'Blessing on you, Silk. Of course you're not bad! You're beautiful and wonderful and all things bright. But you have to understand. Not everyone's like you.

'Some creatures are just wrong – maybe they've been hurt by someone themselves and it's made them shrivel up inside – where their heart should be. And the bright creature The Great God brought into the world is lost and all that's left is a shadow, fuelled by anger and pain and that makes them want to hurt others. Just to make themselves feel better for a while.'

'How are you holding up? Storm's voice was worried.

'My back leg hurts.' Silk coughed. 'A lot ... that thing, whatever it is, has sharp teeth.'

'It's a trap,' Storm told him. 'A poacher's trap. They probably set it to catch rabbits.'

'Well I feel sorry for rabbits!' Silk coughed again. 'And I'm cold ... almost as cold as when I fell through the ice. I keep falling asleep – without any idea I'm going to.'

'We've got to get you out of here.' Storm muttered. He looked at Mistflower. 'You stay here – I'm going for help.'

'All right.'

Mistflower wasn't sure she wanted Storm to leave. If anything went bad while he was gone she would be unable to protect Silk. Besides, what kind of help could he mean? She didn't want to admit it, even to herself, but how could a bunch of animals get Silk out of that thing!

She watched Storm disappear back into the woods. All she could do was put her trust in The Great God and pray all would be well.

Storm tore back through the woods, through the middle field, up the path to the farm house and around to the kitchen. He nudged at the door with his nose but it was firmly shut. Storm started to bark.

Inside the house, Farmer John's daughter, Lucy, paused in doing her homework. Her project was due in the next day, Tuesday, but she had never heard Storm bark like that before. She could tell it was urgent; that something was wrong.

She rushed downstairs, into the kitchen, pulling open the door. 'What is it, Storm? What's the matter?'

Storm ran a few paces away before glancing back at her and giving voice to another round of short, sharp barks.

Lucy could see he wanted her to follow him. She stepped onto the kitchen path. 'Okay boy – where are we going? Show me.'

She followed Storm away from the house, across the field, through the wood and out the other side until he led her to an old elder tree. He stopped, barking and wagging his tail.

'What've you *done!*'

Unnoticed, in the long grass, Mistflower couldn't keep the shock out of her voice. Bringing Farmer John's daughter into this could spell disaster for Silk. Suppose she decided to get her father and he decided he didn't want Silk around. Suppose he decided Silk was past saving and … Mistflower couldn't bear to let herself finish that thought.

'I had to do something, Mistflower!' Storm woofed. 'We'd never have got Silk out of the trap.'

Storm was still barking but Lucy could see nothing wrong. Her eyes searched the ground carefully … there … she'd spotted something, it looked a bit like a log, underneath the tree, covered in brown leaves.

Storm stopped his barking and whined unhappily. He nudged at the pile of old leaves with his nose.

'What've you got there?' She said, curious.

Suddenly she gasped. What she'd thought was a log was actually a black and white cat. He was lying on his side and as she approached he mewed at her silently but he didn't attempt to move. A quick inspection showed her why.

'Poor mite!' Lucy knelt down, stroking Silk's fur. 'Poor little kitty.' She examined the poacher's trap. 'Awful thing! You must be in such pain.'

Lucy knew she had to get the trap open but she was scared to try. What if she couldn't? What if she wasn't strong enough and all she succeeded in doing was hurting the cat more? Perhaps she should go and get her dad?

She was still gently stroking Silk. Unexpectedly, he began to purr. The sound strengthened her resolve. She needed to get that thing open *now* and she was going to succeed and that is all there was to it!

She kept stroking and Silk kept purring. He realised Lucy wanted to help him and he also knew it was the only chance he had.

'I'm going to get this off you,' she told him. 'It – it might hurt – I'll try my best not to let it but – it might. So you have to be brave and trust me. Okay?

Getting a firm grip on the trap, Lucy braced herself ... and ... pulled ... straining hard until, very slowly, the cruel metal jaws began to draw apart.

'Get ready!' Storm barked. 'As soon as there's enough room, drag yourself out of there!'

Slowly, slowly the opening grew and then – as pain flooded into his leg on a tide of misery, Silk drew his leg up, at the same time, using his front claws to drag himself forward on the ground.

Just as he got himself clear of the terrible trap the metal jaws slammed closed again.

Lucy kicked at the thing, 'Curse you and whoever put you there,' she said.

Very gently, she picked Silk up in her arms. Getting to her feet, she began to walk home.

'You're such a good dog,' she told Storm. 'You saw the kitty in trouble and you came to get me – clever, clever dog.' She didn't see the little mouse, running through the grass beside her.

Silk had a long, deep gash, right across his hindquarter. It no longer bled but his whole leg throbbed with a red hot pain and every jolt was torture. Silk didn't care. He understood full well if he had stayed in that contraption for much longer, he would not have survived.

Despite his pain, he was filled with a sense of relief. What happened now he had no way of knowing but he was grateful just to be alive and without those metal teeth biting into him, holding him prisoner, anymore.

As they neared the farmhouse Lucy increased her pace. *'Mum! Mum!'*

Lucy's mother had just come back from the shops and wanted nothing more than a good cup of tea but at the sound of Lucy shouting, she shot out of the kitchen door.

'Lucy! What is it? Are you all right?'

'Mum! I found a cat, caught in a poacher's trap. It's hurt. It's got a big cut on its back leg.'

'Let's have a look.' Lucy's mother came down the path to them.

'Mmm!' She shook her head. 'Those poachers. They don't care what damage they do.' She stroked the top of Silk's head. 'Bring him in love, let's see what we can do.'

Lucy carried Silk inside the house and lay him down on the big, old kitchen table.

'That's a nasty cut – clean down to the bone.' Lucy's mum gently prodded around the wound. We're going to have to take him to the vet. He'll need stitches in that.'

'D-do we have to ask dad first?' Lucy didn't think her dad would want to pay a lot of money to the vet for a stray cat.

'No, love.' Lucy's mother searched out a towel. 'Go and get Peanut's old carry basket. We'll put him in that.'

Lucy breathed a sigh of relief.

'The vet will be able to get Blue Cross or one of those charities to cover the fees and he'll probably do it cheap as well.'

Lucy had been on her way to get the basket. She stopped, turning around. 'Does – does that mean we'll be able to have him back?'

Her mother looked at her thoughtfully. 'Do you want him to come home … to live with us?'

'Yes please, Mum – I – I do. I really, really do.'

'Well, well, little fellow. Aren't you the lucky cat?' She stroked Silk's head again, giving Lucy a big smile. 'In that case – you'd better hurry up with that carry basket.'

Lucy rushed over to her mum, giving her a big hug. 'Thanks, Mum. You're the best.' She dashed away only to return again in minutes with a blue carrier. She stood it carefully on the table beside Silk.

Her mother opened its little door, carefully spreading the towel out. 'There! He'll be comfortable enough on that.'

She lifted Silk, placing him inside, before closing the door securely. 'Come on then – let's get him sorted.'

An hour later they were home again – without Silk.

The vet had told them to come back for him in the morning.

Lucy was not happy. She hadn't wanted to let go of her new cat for one minute, never mind one whole night.

Over supper she told her mum and dad what had led to her finding him.

'Storm's such a good dog,' she told them, glancing over at him where he lay. 'And so clever. He knew the cat was in trouble. He took me straight there.'

'Your mum tells me you want to keep him?'

Lucy nodded, her eyes shining. 'Yes please, Dad. I'll pay the vet's bill. I've got some money saved up and I'll do chores and give you all my pocket money and …'

'Woah! Steady on there.' Farmer John laughed. 'That's very

responsible of you, Lucy. But I'll deal with the bill. You just take good care of the little chap when you bring him home.'

Lucy flung her arms around his neck. 'Thanks Dad!'

* * *

Caramel was feeling decidedly happy as she made her way back to the barn. She had succeeded in getting her life back on track. The mangy kitten had finally been despatched; one down and one to go. And that louse of a mouse would be following it any time now.

The rest of the herd, as well as the other animals in the barn, were all being a bit stand offish at the moment. But she could afford to be patient. In time they would come around. In time they would forget the odd couple ever existed. Yes, Caramel decided, life was sweet. All was well and all would be well.

As she neared home she could see Storm, Lavender, Lilac and the ridiculous rodent standing in front of the barn door. Surely the idiots could see how pointless it was to keep searching for the *thing* any longer? They had to know if they hadn't found him by now it was too late. But they just refused to give up. Well – so what – even if they did succeed in finding him tomorrow or the next day, or the day after that – all they would find would be his empty body.

Caramel would have liked to lift up her tail and run into the barn like a young calf – that's how good she felt. But she schooled herself to a walk, head hanging low, eyes brimming with fake misery.

Abruptly, Storm leapt at her, nipping her hard on the fetlock. At the same moment Lavender butted her.

'*What*?' But Caramel already knew … there was only one possible reason for them to do this.

She started shaking. But how – how could they possibly know? Surely he couldn't still be alive? She would skin that badger herself if she had failed to kill him. She struggled to gather her wits about her. 'What – what are you doing? Have – have you gone mad?'

Storm growled. 'Longtooth confessed. She told us everything.'

Caramel's eyes rolled wildly. 'I – I had to! You don't understand.' She glared at the animals who had gathered around them. 'They – they don't belong here. They're just tramps ... nasty ... f-foul ... creatures.'

'No.' Storm interrupted. 'You're the one who doesn't understand, Caramel. You're the one who doesn't belong here.

'And from this day on, you don't live in the barn. From now on, you'll live in the field with the Bull.'

'*Taurus*! *No*! *Please*!' Caramel pleaded. 'Not that! He – he doesn't even have a pedigree! For pity's sakes! He – he's not even a Friesian and ... and he's *so* demanding. He wants *everything* his own way! And he gets *really* angry if anyone even *tries* to stand up to him.

Caramel's gaze swept over the assembled animals. In their eyes she saw no mercy, not even the slightest trace of pity. She was doomed!

'I – I'll go tomorrow,' she said, edging toward the barn door.

Lavender and Lilac moved to block the entry. They were quickly joined by Dandelion and Cowslip.

Holding back a sob, Caramel slowly turned her back to the warmth spilling out of the barn and stared across at the field where Taurus lived. This time the misery in her eyes was real.

Homecoming

Silk crouched over his water bowl. He could not stop drinking. He couldn't remember ever feeling so thirsty in his life. His bowl was almost empty by the time he limped back over to his blanket.

He was still a little shaky but although his leg was stiff, the raw pain had settled down to a dull ache. If he had to, he thought, as he eased himself down onto his side, he would be able to run. He might even be able to manage a jump ... if his life depended on it.

It was quiet now. There were other cages but they were empty and all the people seemed to have left. He had listened to them talking, he knew in the morning he would be going home. Lucy, that was her name, Lucy wanted him to live with her, in the big house.

Silk was ashamed to say a bit of him wanted that very much. But how could he abandon his friends? How could he abandon Mistflower?

Another bit of him was afraid. Last time he had been part of a family it had all gone bad. Suppose he did live with Lucy? What if everything went wrong again? No, he told himself, humans were not to be trusted. He was better of living with his friends, in the barn, even if it meant having to deal with Caramel.

It was a long time until he finally fell asleep. When he awoke again, it was to the sound of his cage being opened.

Kind hands took him from his temporary home and placed him into the box he had been brought to this place in. He was carried into another room and then he saw Lucy and despite himself, his heart leapt and he heard himself purr as she took the box, lifting him close to her face.

'Hello, Kitty,' she said. 'Let's go home.'

'Welcome back!' Storm yipped as Lucy carried him up the path to the kitchen.

'Storm!' Silk meowed. 'It's good to be back. How's Mistflower? Where is she?'

'I'm here, Silk.'

Silk looked toward where the sound was coming from and spotted Mistflower, well hidden, behind a hawthorn bush.

'Are you all right? Is your leg better?'

'Everything's fine, Mistflower. I'm well.'

Once inside, to Silk's dismay, Lucy carefully closed the door before she let him out of the carrier.

Silk was scared. He didn't like being shut in – away from all his friends – away from Mistflower.

He ran to the door, mewing. He wanted out! He wanted Mistflower.

Lucy crouched down, gently stroking him. 'It's okay, kitty,' she reassured him. 'It's okay. The vet said you've got to stay in until he takes the stitches out – you'll be able to go out then.'

'Just as well,' Lucy's mum said. 'He'll have got used to us by that time. He'll know this is his home and he won't run away when he goes out.

'Let's give him some food and then we'll pop him in his basket. He'll soon settle down.'

The delicious aroma of food drew the starving Silk away from the door and over to a corner of the room where some newspaper had been laid down with a couple of bowls placed on it. Silk made short work of it and very soon he had licked the bowl sparkling clean.

Lucy, who had been watching him, picked him up and carried him to the cat basket, sat next to the warm stove. Silk yawned. The basket looked comfortable and the food was snug in his tummy. He turned around in tight little circles a few times before laying down. Very soon he was asleep.

Silk slept for most of the morning and in between he ate, miraculously, every time he went to his bowl, more food had appeared. When he wasn't eating or sleeping, he fretted. How was he going to escape?

Although it was very nice where he was, he missed his friends, particularly Mistflower. In the barn there was constant coming and going. Here there was only the ticking of the grandfather clock to keep him company.

By afternoon, Silk was more awake. Lucy's mother was working in the kitchen and when Storm barked outside the door she cautiously let him in.

'Storm!' Silk sat up in his basket, pleased to see his friend.

'Careful, Silk.' Storm kept his voice quiet. 'The Missus is watching – she's probably worried I'll go for you.'

'You wouldn't do that!'

Storm wagged his tail, lowering himself down beside the basket. 'But the Missus doesn't know that does she? She can't know I've been sharing my food with you all this time, can she?'

'N-o. I suppose not. I'm not thinking too clearly, am I?'

'I think you're doing just fine after all you've been through.'

'Where's Mistflower? Is she coming to see me?'

Storm whined unhappily. 'The thing is, young Silk, humans, for some reason, don't like mice. If Farmer John or the Missus, or even Lucy saw her, why, they'd like as pitch a fit!'

'But Mistflower's the nicest, kindest, best creature you could ever wish to have as a friend!'

'I know … I know, Silk. But, I'm just telling you how things are – not that that's going to stop her. She told me to tell you she'll come by tonight. When the house is quiet and everyone's in bed.'

'But how will she get in?'

Storm chuffed. 'Don't you worry your head about that.' He got to his paws. 'Right, I'd better get back to the job. Oh – by the way – Mistflower said to give you her love and to tell you to take it easy and to mind your manners.'

He glanced toward the door. 'I'll be back later. You just relax – there's nothing to be afraid of here – they're good people, Silk. There's not many would do what they've done for a stray cat.'

Not long after Storm left, Lucy ran into the kitchen. She came straight to his basket, plopping herself down on the floor next to it. She held her hand in front of his nose. 'It's me boy. It's Lucy. We're going to be best friends you and I.'

Silk suddenly realised he had fallen quite in love with this beautiful young lady who had had enough courage to pit her strength against the terrible steel jaws of the thing that held him trapped.

He kissed her hand over and over again.

Lucy giggled, holding very still. 'Mum – he's licking my hand.'

'I expect he's happy to be warm, fed and safe.'

Lucy said nothing, silently stroking Silk's fur, then. 'His fur's so soft, mum. It's like stroking Silk.' She gazed into Silk's eyes. 'That's what I'm going to call you,' she told him. 'Silk.'

Silk licked her hand again. How clever of this wonderful person – to get his name right. And he hadn't even had to tell her. Silk started to purr. He fell asleep with Lucy still stroking him.

Before he knew it, the day was over. The house was silent except for the grandfather clock ticking in the hall. Silk sat at attention in his basket. He was waiting for his best friend in all the world. He was waiting for Mistflower. He was not disappointed.

Just as the clock struck twelve, Mistflower crept up to his basket. She ran up on top of his head, placing a little mouse kiss on the side of his nose.

'Mistflower!' Silk was overjoyed. Now he finally really felt safe. 'Oh Mistflower, it's so good to see you. I've missed you so much.'

'And I've missed you ten times as much.' Mistflower said, running back down to the ground.

'How – how are you going to get me out of here?'

Mistflower gave him a long, calculating look. 'Don't you like it here?' She asked.

'W-well … y-yes. It's nice … L-Lucy's really kind and so's her mum and Farmer John's nice too.'

'So why would you want to leave?'

Silk ducked his head. 'Well – my place is with you … and … and … in the barn.'

'Your place, Silk,' Mistflower's voice was very soft. 'A cat's place …is in the home. You've found your home now, Silk, and you'd be very silly to leave it.'

'But … what about you? What about …?'

'What about nothing, Silk.' Mistflower touched his paw with her nose. 'Don't you see?' she asked. 'You won't lose a thing … you'll only gain a home and a family. Once your leg is better you can come to the barn as often as you like. You'll be able to spend time with me, with all your friends – and Lucy.

'Think, Silk.' Mistflower insisted. 'No more having to hide when Farmer John comes into the barn. No more having to get better without any help when you're sick. No more being at the mercy of Caramel.'

'But … they won't let you live here.' Silk wailed, miserable.

Mistflower laughed. 'Do you seriously think they can keep me out? Silk, my sweet thing. Mice are not made to live side by side with humans. The Great God made us to be able to slip between the warp and weft of the pattern; in and out of the cracks and holes.

'No – if mice lived side by side with humans they would want to put us in cages. That's how some mice live and I dare say, if it's all they know of life, then they're happy enough. But it's not what we're made for, Silk. And I know what it's like to smell the sweet grass and feel the wind stroking my fur. I've enjoyed the warmth of the Sun on my body and the freshness of raindrops on my nose.

'No – Silk, I could never be happy in a cage. Now!' Mistflower ran up on top of Silk's head again and gave him another little mouse kiss. 'You need your sleep. I'll come again tomorrow.'

Silk was feeling drowsy but he didn't want Mistflower to leave. 'Stay with me for a while?' He pleaded.

'Yes – I'll stay. I'll stay until you're asleep.' Mistflower said, nestling beneath his chin, just the way she always did.

'This is the best place for you, Silk.' She whispered. 'And I'm so happy to see you here and to know, whatever happens, you'll be well taken care of.'

* * *

Very quickly, life for Silk settled into a routine. His leg healed, he regained his strength and found himself able to come and go as he pleased.

Unexpectedly, that Easter it snowed again. Silk spent quite a bit of time sliding down the gently sloping path from the kitchen, before running back to the top and sliding back down again, watched over by Mistflower.

Only a short few weeks ago, he could never have guessed life could be so good. Mistflower had been right when she told him he would lose nothing and gain everything.

He adored Lucy and enjoyed the warmth of the stove and the comfort of his basket on cold nights and during the day, when Lucy was at school, he visited with Mistflower and his other friends to his heart's content.

Gradually the days lengthened and grew warmer.

On the first truly warm day of spring, Mistflower went to lie down underneath the cherry tree, at the bottom of the south field, for her morning snooze. She was often tired these days. Her body felt old and worn and she ached in every bone she had.

This morning everything seemed somehow to be brighter, cleaner, even the air tasted especially fresh. The grass was such a deep, luscious green and Father Sky sparkled above her. A few tiny, fluffy, white clouds sailed slowly by. How soft they looked, Mistflower thought. She wondered briefly how it would feel to lie down on a cloud. Would it be warm or cold? Would it be comforting? Or would it be as if there was nothing there at all?

The Sun was in the heavens with all his splendour and majesty. The earthy smell of the ground rose up and tickled her nose, full of the promise of a good summer to come.

In the hedgerow, creatures were busy building nests and collecting food. Mistflower could hear the soft sounds of their labours and the occasional rustle of leaves.

Reaching the cherry tree, she curled up in the sweet smelling grass with a small sigh. As so often nowadays, a memory of Sage stirred in her mind. For a moment she recalled herself as a young mouse and how the two of them had run and played in the Sun, without a care in the world.

Good days, she thought. Good days and she drifted off to sleep.

'Mistflower!'

Mistflower lifted up her head, her nose twitched. There was something in the air. Something she could not put a name to. And the light, it was so very bright as if a veil had been drawn aside from the Sun. Mistflower could not remember light like that ever before, not even on the warmest summer's day.

'Mistflower!'

The voice was somehow inside her and all around her. It

called to her, but Mistflower was unafraid. There was something familiar about it, something warm and easy and comfortable.

'Come home, Mistflower', it whispered. 'Your nest is ready and those who love you wait.' And suddenly, she understood. For a long moment she fought against that insistent voice.

How could she go and leave behind her all the good friends she had made? How could she go and leave Silk?

'Your work here is done, little mouse. Put down your burden and come home.'

Mistflower sighed softly. Yes ... she was ready.

No more harsh winters to make the ache in her bones into thorns that pierced her limbs and made her long to never have to wake up from sleep. Never again would she have to struggle or fear. Never again would she know hunger.

'Come to me, Mistflower! Come!'

Mistflower gathered herself for one, final, spring and ... she was floating, like a leaf carried in the arms of a warm summer breeze, wrapped in a cloud of light ... and it was soft and gentle and love surrounded her.

The Sun trailed his golden fingers across her fur and the warm spring rain began to fall, covering her with its jewelled beads of life giving water and Mistflower knew the Sun and the Rain had come to keep her company as she began her journey.

They whispered to her of The Great God of All Things love for her as she rose up further and further into the light.

Father Sky unrolled the Rainbow Bridge and Mistflower ran forward eagerly, growing lighter and more joyful with each step.

She ran unhesitatingly toward the light, toward the love and toward the familiar and beloved figure on the other side of the bridge, whom she had missed more than her own heart for time and time.

It had been a long happy, exciting and sometimes difficult journey but now, finally, she was going home.

Old Friends

It was Walpurgis Night in Michaelmas Wood and, as they always did, all the animals had gathered in the clearing to listen to Ghost tell one of his wonderful stories. They had waited patiently all evening, until all other matters were done and now the moment had arrived.

'Hrrumph.' Ghost cleared his throat and paused for an instant before beginning to speak.

'Once upon a time,' he began. 'On a farm close to Michaelmas Wood, lived a very brave, very well loved and very wise mouse. Her name was Mistflower, and this is her story ...'

Afterword

The story of Mistflower was inspired by the many wonderful examples of unusual animal friendships and kindnesses.

Perhaps one of the most unusual is the story of Shooter. Shooter is a four-year-old elk. He stands ten foot tall from his hooves to the tip of his antlers. His keepers at Pocatello Zoo, Idaho, were puzzled to see him trying to dunk his head in his drinking trough, even though his antlers kept getting in the way. Then, to their amazement, he started dipping his hooves into the trough. They were even more amazed when they saw the gentle giant lift a little marmot (a kind of large squirrel) who had fallen into the water, carrying him in his mouth, to place him safely on the ground. Shooter then nudged the little rodent gently with his hoof, as if checking it was still alive, before calmly watching it scamper off.

Not quite so dramatic, though still unusual, is Tom, the cat, who sits on the windowsill each night, awaiting his owner, his paw resting on his best friend's shoulders. The two are inseparable and are constantly together. They sleep cuddled up together, eat side by side and play fight. Nothing unusual there, you're thinking – cats do that all the time – and of course, you're right. Thing is though, Tom's best friend is a leopard gecko.

A good friend of mine has a cat who is best buddies with a gerbil and of course, we shouldn't forget the unusual friendships that exist between humans and all manner of creatures. Ten years ago a very ordinary looking, small, black cat turned up on my doorstep. Honestly, she was not my first choice of a companion, I had no money and it was very clear, after one whiff of her poisonous breath, that she needed urgent dental treatment. However, she was very persistent and the vet generously agreed to monthly repayments. Well, in the end I'm not sure who saved who, but I do know Sweetpea was my best friend and loving companion during a very difficult period in my life.

The spirit of Mistflower is with us always, in the heart of every one of us. Every time we show a kindness to a creature in need, Mistflower is gladdened. She is there for anyone in need of friendship or for anyone just wanting to get in touch and (with a parent's permission) children are welcome to contact her and her friends at (www.mistflowerthemouse.com)

For those children who do write to her, Mistflower has a short story she would love to share with you.

**OUR STREET
BOOKS**

Our Street Books for children of all ages, deliver a potent mix of fantastic, rip-roaring adventure and fantasy stories to excite the imagination; spiritual fiction to help the mind and the heart grow; humorous stories to make the funny bone grow; historical tales to evolve interest; and all manner of subjects that stretch imagination, grab attention, inform, inspire and keep the pages turning. Our subjects include Non-fiction and Fiction, Fantasy and Science Fiction, Religious, Spiritual, Historical, Adventure, Social Issues, Humour, Folk Tales and more.